CW00695028

THE NECESSARY DEATHS

A DELINGPOLE MYSTERY: BOOK 1

DAVID C. DAWSON

PARK CREEK PUBLISHING

ABOUT THE BOOK

The Delingpole Mysteries: Book One

Award winner in the 2017 FAPA President's Awards
for Adult Suspense and Thrillers.

A young man. Unconscious in a hospital bed. His life is in the balance from a drugs overdose.

Attempted suicide or attempted murder?

British lawyer Dominic Delingpole investigates, with the help of his larger than life partner Jonathan McFadden.

Compromising photographs of senior politicians and business chiefs are discovered.

Is the young man a blackmailer?

Dominic and Jonathan uncover a conspiracy reaches into the highest levels of government and powerful corporations.

Three people are murdered, and Dominic and Jonathan struggle for their very survival in this gripping thriller.

This is a work of fiction. Names, characters, organizations, places, events, and incidents are either products of the author's imagination or are used fictitiously. Any resemblance to actual persons, living or dead, or actual events is purely coincidental.

ISBN: 978-1-9162573-0-6

Cover design by: Garrett Leigh @ Black Jazz Design

For Will, who has given me so much support.

1

DOMINIC WOKE with a start. Bleary-eyed, he peered at the glowing digits of the alarm clock on his bedside table. It was half past midnight. As he rolled over to try to go back to sleep, he heard scuffling noises down the corridor of his elegant, ground-floor apartment. He sat up and listened intently. There was something going on outside the front door. The scuffling noises were mingled with the muffled murmur of men's voices. Was someone trying to break in?

After taking a dose of a strong cold remedy to help him fight off a very persistent cold, Dominic had not long fallen asleep. Half-drugged, he stumbled across the bedroom floor. The room was pitch-black, save for the glow of the alarm clock. He gingerly felt his way around the foot of the bed towards the hallway.

The scuffling noise had stopped, but the murmur of the voices continued. The apartment's hallway was lit by the orange glow of the streetlamp outside. An annoying and protracted battle with the local council had failed to turn off this nightly intrusion to the confines of his apartment. As a result, he had got blackout curtains fitted in the bedroom to have any chance of an undisturbed night's sleep. That night, he had forgotten to close them.

As Dominic approached the front door, he contemplated what weapon he had to hand if he needed to fend off an armed intruder. Nothing, save the umbrella in the black-and-chrome art deco stand in the corner and a pair of Chelsea boots sitting on the mat. Perhaps he could simply wedge the door shut with a chair and call the police, hoping they might arrive quickly.

Dominic's apartment was one of six in a large converted Georgian house. As he peered through the spy hole in the middle of his front door, he could see the oak-panelled communal reception hall and the sweeping staircase up to the apartments on the first floor of the house. He could also see two police officers standing over a motionless woman lying on the parquet floor. It was not what he was expecting to see on this wet, wintry night. He unhooked the door chain, opened his front door, and stepped into the hallway to find out what had happened.

Too late he realized that, in his half asleep, half awake state, he was wearing a pair of Dolce & Gabbana low-cut briefs and nothing else. Dominic decided poise and decorum would carry him through this potentially awkward moment. After all, he was in good shape for his thirty-seven years, thanks to three punishing nights a week at the gym. Before him were two young and very cute police officers, and Dominic was temporarily taken aback. They were far more appealing to look at than the woman lying on the floor. Recovering his poise, Dominic held back his shoulders and stood square in the doorway as he asked, "What's going on, officers?"

The two policemen were in their mid-twenties, tall, with close-cropped hair and solid, athletic frames. One was crouched over the woman, putting her into the recovery position, while the other stood a short way from Dominic's open front door about to talk on his radio. If they were surprised by Dominic's sudden semi naked appearance, their faces did not betray it.

"Good evening, sir," said the police officer nearest to him. "We've just had to deliver some bad news to this lady. She fainted and collapsed against your door—I presume the noise woke you? Do you know Mrs. Gregory? She lives upstairs to you."

"Oh my God!" said Dominic. "Yes, she lives in the apartment above me, number four. What was it you had to tell her?"

"I'm afraid it seems her son tried to kill himself tonight," replied the young officer. A voice crackled on his radio. "Excuse me a moment, sir. I'm just raising an ambulance to come and attend to Mrs. Gregory. We're concerned she may have hit her head when she fell."

The police officer spoke into his radio, giving directions to the converted Georgian house in the small market town in rural Oxfordshire. From what Dominic could make out, the ambulance had been dispatched from the nearby John Radcliffe Hospital and was on its way.

He only knew Samantha Gregory to say hello to in the communal hallway. The residents of Ash House kept themselves very much to themselves. He was dimly aware she had a son in his late teens. Dominic seemed to remember her saying he had recently gone away to university in Brighton down on the south coast. She was an attractive, tall woman, probably in her early forties, who was always impeccably dressed. Even as she lay on the polished parquet wood floor, her head turned to one side with the long ringlets of her hair swept back from her closed eyes,

Dominic was struck by her good taste in clothes. It was a sobering reminder of his own current state of undress, and he was about to retreat to his apartment to seek out some more appropriate attire when Samantha stirred and groaned.

"Mrs. Gregory? Mrs. Gregory? Can you hear me?" asked the officer at her side. "No, don't try to sit up. Stay there for a short while. You've had a fall and may have hit your head. Don't try to move just yet."

Dominic seized the opportunity to be more of a useful spectator and less of an undressed interloper on the scene. "Officer, I'll go and fetch a glass of water and a pillow to make her more comfortable."

With that he went back into his apartment, put on an old pair of sweatpants and a sweatshirt that had been hanging on the back of his bedroom chair, and fetched the glass of water from his bedside table. A few moments later, he re-emerged into the communal hallway. He bent down beside the young police officer with Mrs. Gregory. Dominic's eyes lingered for a few moments on the officer's impressive biceps, which were barely restrained by the sleeves of his tunic top. Then he looked back to Mrs. Gregory. Her eyes were open and staring in confusion at the events around her.

"Would you like a sip of water?" Dominic asked. Samantha Gregory pushed herself on one elbow and accepted the glass of water as he raised it to her lips. He noticed there was a large bruise growing darker on her forehead.

"Thank you, sir," said the police officer at his side. "And you are...?"

"Dominic Delingpole. I live at number one," replied Dominic, somewhat redundantly given he had now twice emerged from that doorway. "What's happened to Mrs. Gregory's son?"

"Mr. Gregory is in hospital in Brighton. He survived his attempt to kill himself, but he's unconscious. It looks like he took an overdose, although it's possible it might have been an accident. Fortunately he was found by a housemate, who called the ambulance." A siren sounded in the distance. "Ah, that sounds like our ambulance. Would you mind going out to the street to meet them? It's best that we stay with Mrs. Gregory for the moment."

Dominic crossed the hallway to the main entrance of the house, opened the outer door, and propped it open with a heavy flatiron, left there for this purpose. As he walked out into the freezing night, he realized, again too late, that he was still not properly dressed. The gravel on the driveway cut into the soles of his bare feet as he walked the short distance to the front gate, which opened onto the High Street. A few seconds later, the ambulance rounded the corner at the end of the road. Dominic waved his arms frantically. Then self-consciousness overwhelmed him as he realized he was clearly the only person in the street at that time of night. He reduced his arm waving to a more discreet single-arm-in-the-air, hailing-a-taxi sort of movement. The ambulance drew up, and a green-uniformed paramedic emerged from the passenger door.

"She's in here. Follow me," said Dominic in what he hoped was a firm, assertive voice. The paramedic followed him into the hallway of Ash House. Behind him, his colleague carried an array of medical equipment.

Over the next fifteen minutes, the paramedics assessed Samantha Gregory's condition and announced they would take her to the John Radcliffe Hospital. Dominic turned to her as the paramedics transferred her to a stretcher, and asked, "Is there anything you would like me to do, Mrs. Gregory? Anyone you would like me to call?"

There was a long pause before she responded with a voice that was close to a whisper, "I'm sorry, Mr. Delingpole, this has been a frightful shock to me. I can't believe Simon would do such a thing. He just doesn't do drugs." She looked away as she added, "It's completely unlike him." She turned back to Dominic. "You've been very kind. There's no one else to call at the moment. Simon's father died ten years ago. It's just the two of us, you see." Her eyes brimmed with tears, and Dominic instinctively squeezed her hand.

"Let me give you my phone number, Mrs. Gregory. Do please call me if there's anything I can do. I'm happy to help." He released her hand, went to his apartment, emerged a moment later with one of his business cards, and handed it to her. She glanced at it and said, "Oh yes, I recall you told me you were a lawyer. I have a feeling I might need your services."

2

THE BLACK Mercedes pulled into the makeshift car park, created on a waste ground close to a development area in the City of London. In the backseat, a woman wearing a knee-length coat, its collar trimmed with fur, drummed her fingers on the armrest beside her.

"Why do these people always choose such sordid meeting places?" She pulled her handbag onto her lap and searched for a few moments before producing a lipstick. She looked at the driver in the rear-view mirror. The soft Irish lilt of her voice hardened momentarily. "It's not a rhetorical question, you know. Do me the courtesy of a little conversation, please, while we have to wait in this god-awful place."

The driver slowly passed his hand across his baldhead. She noticed the scar above his temple.

"I've always meant to ask you about that. Now it seems we have time, as he's late yet again. In what particular brawl did you win that trophy?"

The driver looked at her for a moment as though deciding whether to answer or not. Then he spoke. "Chechnya. And what is a brawl?"

The woman ignored his question and started to apply her lipstick, holding the mirror of a small compact close to her face.

The inside of the Mercedes was lit up for a moment as another car entered the waste ground. The headlights of a Range Rover swept past as it turned in a wide arc before drawing up alongside. The woman finished applying her lipstick, took a moment to approve the results of her work, and then packed the lipstick and compact back into her handbag.

She set the handbag on the seat beside her. Finally she turned and pushed a button to lower the window.

"You're late," she said.

"I'm frightfully sorry, ma'am," said a man sat in the Range Rover. "I had a meeting at the House of Commons, and it overran. Nothing I could do to get out sooner."

The woman looked at him contemptuously. "You should reconsider your priorities. We do have others working on the inside there, you know. Now. I'm cold and it's late. So report. Do you have the data card to give me?"

The man shook his head. "They did a thorough search but were unsuccessful. These things are very small, you know. It's very easy for them to be concealed. They were interrupted before they could complete—"

"Well, if they failed to retrieve the data card, is the threat at least neutralized?"

Again the man shook his head. "As I said, they were interrupted—"

The woman raised her hand. "Be quiet. I have to consider whether we elevate this to an international alert now. It's not something I want to happen. Doing that would take it out of my hands. And I'm sure you can appreciate the consequences. Your role would be much diminished. So tell me, can you finish the job?"

The man handed her a thin plastic folder. "I jotted down some notes while I was held up at Westminster. I know how you distrust electronic communications."

The woman took the file. As she rapidly scanned the two pages contained within it, the man continued, "There are complications. The threat is less accessible as a result of what happened. We'll have to adopt a new approach. But I feel confident we can complete the job this time."

The driver of the Mercedes spoke. "I am not confident." The woman looked up.

"Really?" she asked. "What do you propose we do instead?"

The driver shrugged. "It is the wrong technique. It is not a reliable method, as what happened today proves. Let me finish the job. I will succeed."

The woman considered for a moment. Then she looked back at the man seated in the Range Rover. "You've not been very impressive today. Viktor's offer is appealing, but I have other work for him just now. Your man has forty-eight hours to prove himself to us. As do you. Otherwise we'll take matters into our hands. Good-bye."

The window began to rise as the black Mercedes sped off across the waste ground.

DOMINIC WAS in the bathroom, getting ready for whatever the day would throw at him, when his mobile phone rang. Naked, he walked into the bedroom, expecting the morning phone call from his partner, Jonathan.

"Good morning, good morning," he said jauntily.

"Oh, Mr. Delingpole. I'm very sorry to disturb you. It's Samantha Gregory here." Instinctively Dominic reached for the bath towel to restore his dignity—a perverse action, he knew, and one that would have brought an immediate affectionate jibe from Jonathan if he had been there.

"Good morning, Mrs. Gregory. Are you feeling any better after last night? I was so sorry to hear you received such terrible news."

"Yes, it was frightfully embarrassing to faint like that in front of the officers. Fortunately I have only a rather ugly bruise on my forehead and no other lasting effect. I'm just waiting for them to decide whether I can come home today." Her voice faltered on the line.

"Mr. Delingpole?" She paused. "I'm being very cheeky. But I'm ringing to see if you could help me."

Dominic tensed. As a lawyer he could never get used to people who asked for free advice. It annoyed him that they could so casually take him for granted.

"Mr. Delingpole, I have to go to Brighton as soon as possible to see Simon. If they let me out of here today, I'll take the train this afternoon. Could you possibly keep an eye on my apartment for me whilst I'm away? I don't know how long I may be down there, and I'd feel reassured if you would check it occasionally."

Dominic relaxed. Mrs. Gregory was not after free legal advice. Remembering that her son was at one of the two universities in Brighton, Dominic had an idea. Jonathan lived in the town of Lewes, about seven miles along the coast from Brighton. Here was an opportunity for an impromptu visit. Living separately was necessary by virtue of the work they did. Although sometimes Dominic wondered if they used that fact to avoid making a commitment.

"Of course, Mrs. Gregory, that's no problem at all. Which of the two universities is he at? Brighton or Sussex?"

"Brighton. It's very good for journalism and media studies. Simon's very keen on being a journalist. He wants to put the world to rights. God knows, it needs it." Her voice faltered again.

Dominic tried to inject some cheeriness into his voice. "In fact, Mrs. Gregory, I need to be in Lewes tomorrow anyway. I could drive you down later today if that's convenient for you." It was not quite true, but he fancied time away from the office and an evening with Jonathan in Lewes would be perfect.

"Oh, Mr. Delingpole, that's most kind of you, but you really don't need to...."

"It's really no problem, Mrs. Gregory."

"Samantha. Please call me Samantha; this is all too Home Counties formal, given you saw me lying on the floor outside your door last night. Actually, I'd be grateful for the company and the chance to talk about what I'm going to have to do. I may need your advice at some point."

Dominic tensed again.

"I'd pay, of course. I'm not asking for a free ride. But I don't quite know what I'm going to find when I get to Brighton. If you really don't mind taking me down and it's not inconvenient for you, I'd be more than grateful."

And so it was arranged. Samantha would call Dominic when she knew if she could leave the hospital, and he would collect her.

The call ended and Dominic sent a text to Jonathan:

Might be down tonight. Have you got plans? xx

Back came the response:

TV and chocolate.
New Miss Marple *tonight. Bring food. xx*

Dominic and Jonathan had been together for just over two years. It was not easy maintaining a long-distance relationship. To start with, their work had dictated it. Jonathan was a landscape gardener, which in theory he could do anywhere. But Jonathan also played walk-on parts at the world famous Glyndebourne Opera House nearby. He had to be ready for when the occasional summons to perform came, which meant he had to live within a reasonable distance of the opera house.

Jonathan was dismissive of the roles he had played over the years. "Second spear carrier from the left" was how he described his efforts when asked. In fact he had a classically trained tenor voice, a handsome face, piercing blue eyes, and a lean, muscular frame that should have been much in demand in modern opera casting. He was no longer hugely ambitious, or particularly pushy. He had been once, but had not succeeded in getting very far in the fiercely competitive opera world. He loved his landscape gardening, and he felt that, with his occasional appearances on the Glyndebourne stage, it was the perfect combination of work. Most importantly, there was not an office or desk in sight.

By contrast, Dominic, in his own words, "flew a desk." He was most at ease and in command when he sat in his dog-eared leather armchair, either on the phone or talking to clients across his oak desk. The majority of his clientele came from the rural counties around him. He also acted for a few large corporations with smart London addresses. He had first built relationships with them when he was a younger, mildly ambitious lawyer in the City.

He and Jonathan had met at the opera. Their adjoining

picnics on the manicured lawns outside the opera house at Glyndebourne had become somewhat raucous—unusual for the reserved and shy Dominic, but his friends had plied him with champagne to celebrate his birthday. Jonathan described it as lust at first sight, and Dominic had been flattered that such a glamorous and attractive man could have eyes for him. He still felt flattered, but also a little nervous that their relationship might go the same way as his failed, limited liaisons of the past. That was another reason he had so far chosen not to move in with Jonathan. Recently Dominic felt that he wanted the next step to be taken soon. He knew neither of them wanted to broach the subject for fear of upsetting the balance of love and companionship they had achieved.

Was it actually love? Dominic hoped it was, but in truth, with this particular matter, he lacked confidence in the emotions he felt and preferred to allow his cautious, logical mind to manage his personal life.

As HE crossed the communal hallway of Ash House to go to work, Dominic had to pull back to avoid colliding with another resident, running down the stairs two at a time.

"I'm most terribly sorry. I really should slow down. Delingpole, is it?" asked the man breathlessly. "Didn't mean to barge in like that. In a tearing hurry to get to London."

Dominic had met the smartly dressed man very occasionally in the quarterly, interminable residents' meetings. The man rarely attended. He seemed to be constantly traveling. He was a controversial political figure, a Member of Parliament for a constituency somewhere in the north of England. Dominic usually only saw him on television, airing his provocative views on immigration, or how he thought Britain was being so unfairly treated in the world.

"Oh, Mr. James," replied Dominic. "How nice to see you. Are you well?"

Randolph James MP turned his tanned, boyish face to Dominic. "Dear chap, never better. Can't stop now. You must join me for a glass of wine sometime." With that, the flustered MP was out the front door. Even with his tie askew and his hair looking like he had just fallen out of bed, Dominic considered him really something of a catch. It was a shame he was married. Dominic sighed and left Ash House to drive to his small office in the next town.

3

It was shortly after 2:00 p.m. when Dominic's phone rang.

"Mr. Delingpole? It's Samantha Gregory. The doctors have decided I can be let out into the big wide world. Does your kind offer of a ride to Brighton still stand?"

"Oh, of course, Samantha. Shall I come to the hospital now?"

"No, but thank you. I'm getting a taxi back to the apartment. I can't bear to be in this place a moment longer, kind as they are. I only need to pack a few things, so I should be ready soon."

Dominic stood to put on his jacket. "I'm leaving my office now, so I can be home and ready to go in half an hour if you like. Have you found out any more about your son?"

"I telephoned the hospital in Brighton before calling you. He's still unconscious. There's no change. I feel so awful that it's taken me so long to be with him. If I hadn't stupidly fallen last night, I would be there now."

Dominic walked out of the door of his office and turned through the wide gate to the communal parking area. "Well, you'll be there soon. Do you have somewhere to stay in Brighton?"

"I can find a little guest house or something. It is December. I'm sure there'll be lots of vacancies. The English seaside is always rather gloomy in winter, don't you think?"

Dominic resisted offering her the spare room at Jonathan's. For one thing Lewes was nearly half an hour from Brighton, and Samantha had no car. For another he was not particularly open about his relationship with Jonathan in his hometown. He knew it was very old-fashioned of him, and when they were in Lewes, he and Jonathan were known as "the happy couple." But here in Oxfordshire, Dominic preferred to be private and discreet. When he had worked in the City, homophobic remarks had on several occasions slipped from the lips of colleagues or clients he had been meeting. Somehow it was simpler to remain the enigmatic single man.

"I'll come and knock on your door in half an hour, then," was all he said before starting his car.

THEY ARRIVED in Brighton shortly before 6:00 p.m. Dominic kept glancing at the screen of his sat nav to follow its directions to the hospital. He always had it switched to silent, as he found that with the volume turned up, the cold, authoritarian commands broke into all conversation in the car. When he was alone, it would be an unwelcome interruption to his stream of thought. He occasionally missed a turning, but at least it was preferable to being shouted at by a soulless computer voice.

It was a very cold, wet, and windy evening in Brighton.

The rush hour traffic moved slowly as the car inched towards the eastern end of the city and the Royal Sussex County Hospital.

"I'm sure parking is going to be an absolute nightmare when we get there, Dominic," said Samantha. The journey had given them time to relax formality on both sides. "So why don't you just drop me at the entrance and then you can get on to your friends." Despite relaxing formality Dominic had still not been forthcoming about Jonathan.

"Well, I'm not due to see them until seven, so I'll just come in briefly with you. You're only just out of hospital yourself; I really don't want to simply leave you on the doorstep. I can ring around and find you a place to stay while you see your son and talk to the hospital staff. I'm sure it's not going to be very easy for you."

Samantha turned to him and rested her hand briefly on his left thigh. "Dominic, that's very kind. I won't say no." She turned to look out of the window, perhaps to hide the emotion in her eyes. "At the moment, I really don't know what I'm going to do next." She lifted her hand from his thigh and pointed to a turning up ahead.

"There it is. The sign says the car park is over to the left. Let me find some coins. This rain is just ghastly." She busied herself with the practical matter of searching for her change purse in the depths of her handbag. Then she looked up. "Two hospitals in twenty-four hours. It's really not a very good record, is it?"

THE SHORT walk from the car to the main entrance of the hospital left them damp and cold. Dominic followed

Samantha as she led the way to the ward where the receptionist at the main desk had said her son had been admitted. As they waited at the ward's reception desk, she turned to him. "Dominic, would you mind awfully coming with me? Just for a moment? I'm sure I'll be fine, but...."

A nurse standing next to them interrupted her. "Mrs. Gregory? I'm one of the nurses in charge of your son. We moved Simon up to the ICU half an hour ago. I'm afraid he got a little worse, but it's just a precaution. His kidneys are having a bit of a struggle at the moment," she added. "Let me take you there now."

Samantha swayed slightly, and Dominic put his arm around her waist to stop her from falling. "I'm here," he said. "Come on, let's see him now."

The nurse took them to the staircase and up to the second floor of the building. The Intensive Care Unit occupied the whole of the floor of this wing. Patients had their own rooms, festooned with electronic equipment. In the third room to their right was Simon Gregory. Through a glass wall, they could see his face covered by an oxygen mask, his bare chest wired to flashing monitors, and a drip attached to his right arm. Sitting at Simon's bedside was a young man with a mop of curly hair, wearing a torn T-shirt and jeans.

"He was doing quite well until about half an hour ago," said the nurse in a low, sympathetic tone. "Then his kidneys seemed to be having a little difficulty, so we brought him up here, just as a precautionary measure. We'll see how he goes in the next twenty-four hours. His friend's with him at the moment, and I'll have to ask him to leave while you're here. Patients can't have more than two visitors when they're in the ICU. Wait here while I speak to him."

The nurse entered the room, and as the door swung open, they heard the multiple beeps of the machines hooked up to Samantha's son. A few moments later, the nurse emerged with the curly-haired young man.

"Hi, Mrs. Gregory. I'm John Fraser, one of Simon's housemates. It was me who found him yesterday. I'm very sorry." The young man's voice was flat and monotone. He looked tired, and Dominic thought his eyes were probably red from crying.

"Thank you so much, John, for being with him," said Samantha. "I'm so grateful for what you've done. You don't have to leave now. You can come in again with me if you like. This is Mr. Delingpole. He has an apartment downstairs to mine. He's been kind enough to bring me down in his car, but he's leaving now to go meet with his friends.

"Thanks, Mrs. Gregory, but I ought to get back to the house," replied John. He stood up and dragged a battered leather jacket from the back of his chair. "I need to tell the others what's been happening. I'll come back again tomorrow when I've had a bit of sleep." Before he left, he exchanged phone numbers with Samantha.

She turned to Dominic. "You really don't need to stay any longer. You've done so much for me already. Off you go. I'll let you know when I have some news." She reached forward to kiss him gently on his cheek; then she looked back through the window at her son as she said, "Believe me, Simon doesn't take drugs, and he wouldn't try to kill himself. I know my son."

Dominic watched as she entered the room and leaned across Simon's unconscious body to kiss him tenderly on his forehead. Much as he admired Samantha's loyal support of her son, Dominic wondered if she really knew Simon as well as she claimed. Perhaps his mental state had changed since he became a student. But then, perhaps her conviction that he was not just another attempted suicide statistic was more than simply blind faith.

4

As Dominic left the hospital, he spotted Simon's roommate emerging from the shop in the main entrance with a bottle of water in his hand.

"Can I offer you a ride somewhere, John?" Dominic asked. "You must have been through a lot in the last day."

"Thanks. I... Well, actually. Yeah. That would be great if it's not too much trouble for you. The buses here are crap. I don't live nearby. It's a bit of a hike. The house is beyond Kemp Town. Yeah. Thanks. I mean, I'd be very grateful."

The rain had stopped, but the wind seemed to be getting stronger as they headed across the car park to Dominic's Audi convertible. As soon as Jonathan had seen it he christened it "Dominic's Diana", acknowledging it was the preferred car of the late Princess. For Dominic, the car was an indulgence he had never regretted.

"How long have you known Simon?" he asked by way of conversation as they closed the car doors against the winter wind.

"We've been sharing the house since the start of term," replied John. "There are four of us. We got put together.

We're the outies— out of halls. We didn't get places in a hall of residence, so we're in this rented house. It's not bad, but a bit grubby. Don't think my mum would approve—if she ever got to see it.

"We're all doing way different courses. Simon's doing journalism and media studies, which seems like a complete doss, and I'm doing biochemistry. Then there's Gemma doing English, and Jay, who's doing a postgrad in pharmacology. We've all really hit it off, thank God, although we hardly see Jay. He's often working late here at the hospital. Si's the resident joker. I think he's a frustrated drama queen. He's a great guy—really great guy." John broke off, as though he was about to say more but chose not to.

Dominic decided to change the subject. "You're going to have to give me directions. How far beyond Kemp Town is it?"

John peered through the windscreen at the rain-washed road they were following. "Take the second left down there and then the first right into Green Street. There's a fiddly turning, and then it's our street."

Dominic negotiated the narrow suburban streets crammed with terraces of neat little houses. After a few hundred yards, he turned the car into a shabby street of larger, run-down Victorian terraced houses.

John pointed to a house up ahead. "Ours is the one with the skip outside. The people opposite are using it to dump the crap in from their building work. It seems to be a permanent feature. Thanks a lot. Cool car by the way." He was unbuckling his seat belt when he turned and asked, "How do you know Simon's mum?"

Dominic pulled up outside the house. "We live in the same block of apartments. When she got the news last night, I thought it was the least I could do to bring her down here. She's very upset, even though she appears quite calm."

"Yeah, I'm not surprised. This isn't Simon. He doesn't do this stuff. He's not suicidal. He doesn't do drugs. I know it sounds weird, but none of us do. I mean, the occasional smokes, but not what they're saying Simon took. He didn't do it, I know." John turned to Dominic and looked him straight in the eyes. "I know Simon. This isn't what he'd do."

"Then what do you think happened?" asked Dominic. "I presume it's the police who are saying he took the overdose?"

"Yeah, the paramedics and the police all kind of came together. The police have questioned us all, and the hospital says they pumped out his stomach. But it's all wrong. There's never been any stuff in the house like that. I know that." John stopped as he had before, as if he wanted to say more but was holding back. "Look, I'd better go and talk to the others. Thanks for the ride. I'll go and see Simon again in the morning."

John jumped out of the car, slammed the door, and was gone. Dominic waited to see John safely inside the house. He reflected that it was quite normal for John to refuse to believe his friend had tried to kill himself. But John's insistence seemed to go much further. There was something he seemed to be avoiding saying, and now Dominic was curious. He put the car into drive and headed back to the main road and Jonathan's little hilltop Victorian terrace in Lewes. The last forty-eight hours had been unusually eventful for Dominic, and he badly needed a glass of wine.

"FIRE'S LIT and the wine's open. What did you bring for

supper?" Jonathan's voice boomed from the kitchen as Dominic opened the front door.

"I'm afraid it's not very imaginative," Dominic replied. "Mussels and French bread. I hope you've got some decent salad because it all looked a bit sad in the supermarket."

Dominic put down his overnight bag and paused to absorb the warmth of the fire as Jonathan entered the small front room. "Perfect, lover. Lettuce and tomatoes left over from the Glyndebourne kitchen and the last of our garden radishes. A feast!" He wrapped his left arm around Dominic's neck and planted a kiss full on his lips, at the same time grabbing Dominic's crotch with his right hand. "I'll pour you a glass of pinot while you take the weight off your feet and tell me about all the excitement."

Jonathan was a complete contrast to Dominic. Loud, large, and not at all inhibited. Dominic loved and admired his partner's ability to embrace life and ignore the hurdles it seemed to throw in his path.

For life had not been easy for Jonathan. His mother died when he was just two and his traditionalist religious father gave up the struggle of parenthood soon after. Jonathan was taken into care, and a succession of foster parents helped him develop a strong sense of independence and an expectation that relationships always failed. He left the last of his foster parents at the age of sixteen and moved from Sussex to London, where he lived a life rich in experiences, more than a few of them sexually dubious.

His singing voice was to be his passport to a career. By age twenty-one, he was working in a Soho bar that was popular with the opera going crowd.

When Jonathan did the morning clean up of the bar, he would replace the cheesy 70s mix tape on the stereo with his own recordings of Puccini operas and sing along to them. One morning the music director of the London Symphony Chorus walked in and took a shine to both Jonathan and his raw tenor voice. Reginald Hanes CBE offered to coach Jonathan and also offered him a room in his grand but faded London Marylebone apartment. Jonathan accepted and moved in. Within three months he was a member of the chorus and within six months was auditioning for roles with the principal opera companies in London.

His relationship with Reginald Hanes did not last, however, and the auditions failed to bring Jonathan much more than small and sporadic chorus parts. After nearly three years of struggle, he decided to turn his back on London and return to the south coast, where he got a job working in the gardens at the Glyndebourne Opera Company. Finally he found contentment. He discovered that he loved gardening, and the director of the opera company was grateful to have someone he could call on at short notice to understudy for the chorus.

As Dominic sat by the fire and removed his shoes, he looked again at the sepia photo of a laughing, carefree woman standing on the cliff top at Saltdean. It was the only photo Jonathan had of his mother, but there was a copy of it on display in every room of the little cottage. A curious obsession, but one that Dominic understood.

"So who is the mysterious woman, then?" called Jonathan from the kitchen. "She must have some charm for you to break with routine and come down here midweek." Jonathan emerged with two glasses and a bottle. "Wonderful of course that you are here, my dear." He put the glasses down on the table, poured a generous measure of wine, and handed it to Dominic. "Cheers, my dear. It's very good to see you. Is she going to be a rich benefactress who will save your ailing law practice and bring us riches beyond our belief?"

Dominic recounted the events of the night before and his unsatisfactory conversation with John in the car. "So it's all rather strange," he concluded, "although probably easily explained as an emotional student's experiment with drugs that went wrong."

"But you don't think so, do you? And it's one thing I've learned about you in our glorious two years together: your instincts are rarely wrong, if not a little infuriating on occasions. For someone who spends their time on legal logic, I've never quite understood how you can bear to give yourself over to raw gut feeling." Jonathan squeezed onto the sofa alongside Dominic and put an arm around his shoulder.

Dominic bristled and retorted, "Intuition and instinct are merely the superior level of your brain drawing conclusions based on the stimuli of multiple senses. We supposedly rational adults spend too much time relying on what we consider to be intellect—"

"Oh my! I feel a Dominic moment of didactic discourse coming on," teased Jonathan, but Dominic was now in full flight.

"—by ignoring our intuition and instincts, we risk ignoring the sensitivity that we can have to the way other people behave, particularly those we love. But because we are unable to articulate this sensitivity, we so-called intellectuals...."

Jonathan sighed and removed his arm.

"We so-called intellectuals," continued Dominic, "too often forget that mothers know their children instinctively. Samantha is a sensitive person; there wasn't a moment when she doubted her son, or thought he was in the wrong.

She didn't once say, 'what if I'm wrong?' And then there's John."

"Ah, the housemate. Are they lovers, do you think?" mused Jonathan.

"Why is it that you automatically think all men are gay?" asked Dominic in frustration. "Or is it simply that you wish they were?"

Jonathan ignored the jibe. "You did say he seemed upset when you first arrived. Perhaps he's formed some kind of attachment, even if it's not reciprocated. Male teenage adulation is very common you know, even in boys who grow into full-blooded alpha males. Or maybe it's a guilt thing. Maybe...," he went on, warming to a theme. "Maybe he's the drug taker in the house, and he persuaded young Simon to try something. The experiment went horribly wrong, and now Simon's in a hospital ward and John's got the police breathing down his neck."

Dominic took a sip of wine. "John said that none of them took drugs in the house. And he told me in a way that I believed. It was almost naïve the way he said it, but very credible."

"Is this your instinct kicking in again?" asked Jonathan. "You know I love you for it, but there seems to be a distinct lack of hard facts here just at the moment. We don't even know what the young man overdosed on. Come on. You're the lawyer, I'm the artist. I shouldn't be the one telling you that you need more facts. You've got me completely intrigued, and you're simply going to have to find out a lot more. Do you have to dash back to Oxfordshire tomorrow morning? Can't you find some reason to meet up with the mysterious and captivating Samantha again?"

Dominic reflected for a moment. "I can't help thinking there's much more to this than a student's moment of madness. I'm supposed to be seeing that awful client with his patent dispute tomorrow afternoon, but I could put him off until Thursday."

Dominic's caseload, working in a provincial legal practice, had brought him a respectable income for several years. But work had declined recently. He knew it was down to something they called "dynamic marketing"—two words he dreaded. He felt anything but dynamic, and he hated the thought of marketing himself. He knew he was going to have to do something about it soon, but he had lost the ambitious hunger of his youth.

His choice of a career in commercial law had started promisingly. After a first in history at Oxford, he had sailed through his law college exams and secured an internship with a prestigious London firm. But all too soon Dominic got bored. His clients' legal battles over large sums of disputed money were for him esoteric and simply greedy. He felt unfulfilled. Weekend walks in the Chiltern Hills near Oxford gave him the inspiration to move to a country practice. The pace was slower and the work was more varied, if less well paid, and his colleagues in the small market town legal practice were altogether more pleasant and, well, gentlemanly.

That feeling of contentment had lasted for more than seven years. Then he met Jonathan, who brought a new sense of fun and excitement into his life. Dominic felt dull and sedentary by comparison with his happy-go-lucky companion. It was time for a change, but he had yet to work out what form the change would take.

"I'll drop an e-mail to Gillian to clear my diary for tomorrow. Why not? The clients can wait one more day. Samantha did say she might have need of my services. I'd hate to appear like an ambulance chaser, but...."

"But she's woken up the macho male in you, and you're intrigued," Jonathan said as he stood up, glass in hand. "My dear, it will be the second impulsive decision you've made in twenty-four hours. It's a first, and something to celebrate. Now come through to the kitchen, or the mussels will be steamed to extinction."

5

DOMINIC WAITED until the next morning to send a text to Samantha. He took time to phrase it carefully. On the one hand, he had genuine concern for her situation, but he was also conscious that his concern, coming from a lawyer, could be misconstrued as fishing for business. But what the hell, he was already painfully aware of his present lack of dynamic marketing skills.

Whatever fears Dominic had were dispelled when he received a text reply almost by return. It read:

Meet me at the hospital at 11. I need to ask your advice.
Samantha x

Jonathan left early for a meeting about a landscaping project with a wealthy client who had recently taken over a rambling old manor house in acres of land on the South Downs. "She's totally crazy, my dear, but loaded. If she pays the bills, then we can spend Christmas in Rio," he said cheerfully before leaving at seven thirty that morning.

In Dominic's e-mail to his secretary, he not only asked

her to clear his diary for that day, but also to field all his calls and ensure he was not disturbed. Like many experienced legal secretaries in small provincial firms, Gillian was more than capable of dealing tactfully with the demands of self-important clients. She was very fond of Dominic, and she was also the only person in the firm who knew the truth of his relationship with Jonathan. A mother of two grown daughters, she treated Dominic as the son she had never had and was often a source of advice, invited or otherwise.

Dominic decided to drop by the shared student house where John lived on the way to the hospital. He was not sure what he might achieve by the unannounced visit, but at the very least, he felt he could discover more about the background to Simon's daily life.

As he walked up the path of the dilapidated Victorian house in Lowell Street, the front door burst open, and a young woman wrapped in several layers of clothing flew out, almost colliding with him.

"Oh my God, I'm so sorry!" she said, clutching his arm as her feet skidded on the icy path. Her hair was braided in dreadlocks, and she wore a large pair of headphones. She slipped them off her ears and around her neck, looked at him more closely, and added, "Are you from the police? Only I'm supposed to be in a lecture at nine, and I'm late already, so if you want to ask any more questions, could I do it later?"

"Oh, no, I'm not from the police. I was actually looking for John, but I suppose he might be at a lecture as well. I gave him a ride back from the hospital last night and—"

"So you're the one with the flash car with the leather seats! John was well impressed. No, he's still in. Not sure he's going in to uni today. He's still really cut up about Si. Look, I've got to go, but hang on—I'll let you in." The young woman turned back to the front door and opened it with her key. "John!" she shouted into the house. "That guy's here who gave you a ride. John?" There was a muffled response from the gloomy depths of the stairwell.

"I think he'll be down in a minute," she assured him. "Wait in the warm. It's freezing out here. Mind you, it's not much warmer in there. Heating's on the blink. I'm Gemma, by the way." She held out a hand enveloped in a large woollen glove, and they shook somewhat formally.

"Got to go. Great to meet you," and she disappeared down the path. Dominic stepped into the hallway, and the front door slammed shut behind him. A smell of damp mixed with the slightly sweet smell of rancid carpet greeted his nostrils. The hallway was only slightly warmer than the icy December day outside. He thought back to his student days in Oxford and was grateful for the comfortable, if smothering, college rooms he had lived in at Exeter College.

A pile of unopened post lay on the threadbare carpet by the front door, together with three pairs of scruffy trainers, a bicycle wheel, and a row of empty bottles. Dominic bent down and picked up the letters. Being somewhat obsessive about tidying, he began to sort the advertising circulars from what looked like the regular post. There were three letters for Simon Gregory, one marked University of Brighton and two others marked with the logo of the drug company Barton Kane. As Dominic turned the envelopes idly in his hand, a voice came from the landing above.

"Mr. Delingpole, hi. I didn't know you were coming over." Dominic looked up to see a sleepy-eyed John, wrapped in a duvet, standing at the top of the stairs. The dishevelled figure began to walk down.

"I was sleeping in this morning as I've only got a tutorial at two," John said. "Do you want a coffee or something?

There's probably no milk. Do you mind it black?" The young man stopped at the foot of the stairs and eyed the handful of half-sorted post in Dominic's hand.

Dominic suddenly felt guilty holding the household's post, as though he might be suspected of stealing it. "Don't worry about the coffee, really. I just came over to see how you were. I'm on my way to the hospital, and I just thought I'd drop in."

John yawned and hung on the newel post at the bottom of the stairs. "I'm okay, thanks. Bit hung-over, actually. The others thought I needed a bit of cheer last night, so they topped me up a bit with some alcohol. I'm going to have a coffee. Otherwise I'll never make it in to uni today."

He slipped past Dominic and along the corridor to the back of the house. Dominic followed him into a dingy 1970s-style kitchen with a grubby floor, overflowing worktops, and several cupboard doors hanging from their hinges.

"Excuse the mess. It's not Friday yet," said John as he dug out a couple of mugs from a pile of dirty dishes in the sink and rinsed them under the tap. "Friday's the day we blitz the house in readiness for the weekend, when it gets trashed again," he added by way of explanation. "Are you sure you won't have a coffee? It won't take a second."

Dominic was not fond of instant coffee but thought it would be churlish to turn down John's hospitality, despite the state of the mugs.

"Well, maybe just a half. There are a couple of letters for Simon here. I could take them to Samantha this morning if you like."

"Sure. Actually, you could take a couple of other things in for him. They say coma patients should be surrounded by familiar stuff. I was going to take his iPod to the hospital yesterday but forgot. I thought that if they played his music to him, it might nudge him somewhere deep down. Hang on a minute. I'll go and get it." John tipped a heaped spoonful of coffee into each damp mug before disappearing up the stairs.

Dominic wrinkled his nose as he looked around the beige-painted kitchen. There was a Formica-covered breakfast bar strewn with a mix of study papers and the remains of a takeaway curry. The walls were decorated with posters from several student drama productions and revision notes on the subject of Brecht.

John returned, no longer clutching the duvet but dressed in a pair of shabby sweatpants and a singlet. He handed a small plastic bag to Dominic. "Do you mind? It's Si's iPod, headphones, charger, and some photos of us—the house, that is. We had a party the other week, and it got a bit crazy. Si was on good form and we took loads of pictures. I printed some off at uni. If you could...."

Dominic took the bag, opened it, and dropped the three letters for Simon into it. "Of course. It's no problem." He watched as John busied himself with the coffee for a moment. "Look, John. It's really not any of my business, and you can tell me that if you want. But just how well do you know Simon?"

John turned around. "What do you mean?" He looked at Dominic with a startled look on his face.

"I think you know what I mean," said Dominic. You're very close, aren't you?"

John looked away. "Si's mum doesn't know anything about us. He wasn't ready to tell her. I don't want you to go blurting stuff out to her. Look...." He turned back to Dominic. "I'm his first boyfriend. It kind of happened the first week we arrived in the house. He was really shy about it all at first and didn't want the others to know. He said he'd known for a while, but meeting me...." Tears welled in his eyes. "He's an amazing guy, and we were—we are—incredibly happy. There's no way he was thinking of killing himself."

Dominic resisted the impulse to give John a comforting hug, conscious of his professional standing and the fact that it would embarrass them both. He thought back to the night before and what John had called the residents of this shared student house: the outies. In John and Simon's case it was suddenly a very appropriate choice of word, he thought.

"We have to be practical here, John," Dominic said. "If the police continue their investigations, which they will, then they'll start to dig deeper into Simon's personal life. Think about it. Do you really want the police revealing the reality of your relationship to Mrs. Gregory? It could be a much more difficult surprise for her."

John said nothing and stared at the floor. Finally he looked back at Dominic. "I don't know. It was up to Si. I can't break a promise to him, even after what's happened. Not yet anyway. Maybe if...." He broke off, as if not wanting to say the unthinkable.

Dominic decided to take command.

"It's all right, John. You're right to respect Simon's wishes, so you should say nothing for the moment. Besides, Mrs. Gregory has quite enough on her mind as it is. But the question remains, how did Simon come to take a drugs overdose? You say this household is drugs-free, but you did say last night that you took 'the odd smokes.'"

John opened his mouth to say something, but Dominic, now in full flow, continued, "Look. Both you and Mrs. Gregory seem convinced that Simon's not the type to commit suicide. Lots of people have said that about friends and loved ones who kill themselves, but for some reason I think there's more to this. John, I'm not the police. Why don't you tell me exactly what happened when you discovered Simon?"

John took a long pause and looked hard at Dominic. Then it was as though a switch had been flicked.

"I'm usually the last one back to the house in the evening. Because of the labs I have to do in the afternoon. Si doesn't seem to have many lectures at all. I always say it seems like a bit of a doss. Gemma—she let you in this morning—she does English, and that seems just as dossy. She's only got to be in a few days each week. Me and Jay—he's the one doing the postgrad in pharmacology—we're the ones who seem to work the hardest.

"Anyway, Si was supposed to be meeting a guy about a summer job he wanted with some flakey production company here in Brighton. He's desperate to get into TV. Then he sent me a text to say that the guy had blown him out. He said he was coming back here and why didn't I come back early too? It seemed like a great idea as my lab was all going wrong, so I got the next bus.

"When I got back here and went upstairs, Si was lying facedown on the bed. He was naked, and I thought for a moment it was like a come-on, but then...." John paused for a deep breath. "He was just completely still. His breathing was normal but like, really slow. I couldn't wake him at all. Then I saw he'd thrown up, and I was dead panicked that he could choke if it happened again, so I checked his airway and got him into a recovery position and covered him with some bedclothes and then called the ambulance."

The young man seemed to be exhausted from the effort of telling his story, and he paused, his chest rising and falling in rapid, shallow breaths.

"I'm sorry," said Dominic. "I'm sure you've said all this to the police already. Do you want to stop?" He put an arm around John, who turned and buried his head in Dominic's shoulder.

"No," he said quietly. "This is the first time I've felt just how shit it was. I've never felt so desperate in my life before." He held his head up and wiped his eyes. "You see, before the paramedics arrived, that was when I found the K."

Dominic loosened his arm from John's shoulder. He knew that K was short for ketamine, an anaesthetic used by vets. It was also an increasingly common recreational drug. "Did you show it to the paramedics?"

John looked guiltily at Dominic. "I panicked. I thought that if they knew it was there, the police would smash the place up looking for other stuff."

"You know that it would have helped the medics, don't you? Your actions in withholding that information have made it harder for them to know the best way to treat Simon. Quite possibly it could have endangered his life. You may still have threatened his long-term chances. And anyway, they'll find traces of the ketamine when they do his toxicology tests."

Dominic was about to pull out his phone to call the hospital, but there was the sudden thunder of feet on the staircase, and a moment later a tall Adonis of a young man burst into the kitchen. He was wearing a pair of knee-length basketball shorts and nothing else. His broad shoulders framed an impressive pair of bronzed pectoral muscles.

"Who's this?" the Greek god asked John. "Another fucking copper?" Without pause he walked over to the fridge, opened the door, and began to drink from a carton of milk.

"This is Dominic Delingpole, the friend of Si's mum

who brought me home last night. Dominic, this is Jay."

"Ah, the postgraduate in pharmacology. I'm pleased to meet you." Dominic extended his hand while trying hard not to stare, but Jay ignored him and continued to drink his milk.

"Shit, Jay, you don't have to be so rude. Mr. Delingpole's been really helpful. He's taking Simon's stuff up to the hospital now."

Jay put down the now empty carton of milk. "Sorry, mate, but I've just about had it with the fucking British police in the past forty-eight hours. They reckon that because I'm doing pharmacology, I must be shovelling the stuff up my nose all the time. I'm sure it's not going to be long before they're back to rip this place apart with their sniffer dogs." There was a strong Australian twang to Jay's voice. Wherever he was from, he knew how to create a perfect physique. Dominic admired the muscles that rippled across Jay's tanned body.

"It's not so surprising the police suspect a houseful of students of possessing drugs when one of them seems to have overdosed." Dominic looked across to John.

John's face flushed briefly, but he simply replied, "Thanks for taking the stuff up to the hospital for Si. Do you want to get off now?"

Dominic picked up the small bag of Simon Gregory's things and headed for the door. Then he turned to Jay.

"So if you're doing pharmacology, why would it be that Simon, the media student, is getting letters from Barton Kane, the drug company?" he asked, showing Jay the two letters he had picked up in the hallway earlier.

Jay's deep blue eyes stared back unblinking at Dominic. "Well, he's got to pay the bills like the rest of us."

"What do you mean? Was he working for them?"

"Kind of. Look, lots of students do it. They need money, and the bastard drug pushers like Barton Kane need guinea pigs for their trials. Barton Kane's signed up quite a few in Brighton over the last two years. I should know. I am one. It was Simon Gregory who recruited me."

Dominic took a deep breath. "Do the police know this?"

Jay shrugged his shoulders. "Why should they? There's nothing illegal about it. Ethics and morality, well, that's another thing. You give most of your rights away with the contract they get you to sign."

"Does Simon's mother know he works for Barton Kane?"

This time there was a pause before Jay answered. "I can't believe she does for a moment. But then, I've never met her. Si doesn't say much about her. They're not close."

"What sort of drug was Barton Kane testing?" asked Dominic.

"I can't tell you. Really. They just got Si to recruit people of the right sort. Apparently pretty well all the guinea pigs are male, but we're different ages, different ethnic backgrounds. It's all dead secret and commercial confidential. All we have to do is take the drugs and fill out our log cards."

"Log cards?"

Jay reached into his pocket and drew out a small pale blue card. It had Jay's name on the front, followed by a column of tick boxes.

"They give us these to fill out, one for each day. You take the pill, then report how you feel every eight hours. It's a fucking pain in the backside. Still, it pays well. And when you're struggling for cash, you take the risk."

Dominic was about to leave when a thought struck him. "You called them bastard drug pushers a moment ago. Aren't you going to be joining their ranks soon if you're studying pharmacology?"

Jay smiled, and Dominic was treated to a flash of perfectly white and expensive orthodontics. "Not if I can help it, mate. As soon as I'm finished here, I'm going back to Sydney and joining the police. I want to get into forensics there, if they'll have me. I'm not going to be owned by Barton Kane or any of the other bastards either."

"Shit, Jay," John exclaimed. "You're either in or you're out. You're happy to take their money now while you need it, then you claim some kind of high principle. Shit, and you call us whinging."

John's outburst surprised Dominic. Its vehemence seemed rooted in some history between the two young men, and yet John had told him in the car yesterday how they all got on really well.

Jay simply smiled. "I'd shut your mouth, little prom queen. After all, you've done all right from them as well. A bit of sponsorship on your biochemistry course hasn't hurt you. Why are you defending them? Paying you well, are they?"

"All I'm saying is, you don't have to whine about it if you're going to take their money." John turned to Dominic. "I know Si hasn't told Mrs. Gregory about Barton Kane so far. It's not anything to worry about—they test all this stuff on animals first—"

"And on poor bastards in the Third World," interrupted Jay.

"—so probably best not to worry her any more just for the moment. The hospital will know, and if they decide to tell her, then fine," continued John.

Dominic left the house, his head reeling with all the new information he had just learned. One thing was certain: a few extra, unplanned days' stay with Jonathan was now a distinct possibility, and one he found very appealing.

6

———

It was shortly before eleven when Dominic arrived at the Royal Sussex County Hospital. He sat in the car and rang Gillian to check his messages and tell her about his plans to stay on.

"Don't worry, I can manage everything here, Dominic. It's quiet at the moment. You have that High Court hearing next week and the documents to put in for the Cunningham case, but those are the only pressing matters." Gillian's voice changed, betraying her motherly instinct. "Is everything all right?"

Her question made Dominic pause. He discussed most things with her, but now was not the time.

"It's fine. I just wanted a little time out of the office, and Jonathan's not frantically busy just now." It was almost true. "I may be picking up a new client anyway, so it's partly business, although what I can do for her, I'm not quite sure yet."

"Well, as long as you're both well. Are you going to be back in time for that grand dinner at Chequers? It's in three days' time. Let me know if you want me to send your apologies."

He had completely forgotten about his invitation to dinner with the prime minister. Dominic's apartment was only a few miles from Chequers, the weekend retreat for whoever was prime minister of the day. It was an impressive Tudor-style building with Gothic overtones. Over the centuries it had played host to many British prime ministers, including Churchill. Lady Jane Grey had once been imprisoned there. Dominic had walked past it on several country rambles and had often wondered what it would be like to step inside. Now was his chance. "Oh, I'll definitely be back in time. I wouldn't want to miss that opportunity."

"You seem very keen to be at something that is really just the local chamber of commerce sucking up to the prime minister. I didn't know you were a supporter of this present regime," Gillian said suspiciously. Dominic knew of her fierce opposition to the current government, mainly based on its plans to slim down the National Health Service and introduce more private health care. Gillian was a lifetime socialist. Dominic avoided political discussions with her, and in return Gillian had dismissed him as a soggy liberal.

"Oh, I wouldn't call myself a supporter," he said hastily. "But it will be interesting to see the inside of the place after all these years of living so close by. I'll try and smuggle out a hand towel with a crest on it for you, as a souvenir."

"Theft, Dominic?" asked Gillian sternly. "I don't think a man in your position should be considering that. I presume Jonathan knows? You remember that the invite said partners are included?"

Jonathan had yet to accompany Dominic to any formal event in Oxfordshire. Of course when he had casually mentioned the invitation, Jonathan had jumped at the chance, saying that he would drop anything to be there.

"Yes. Jonathan's not stopped talking about it since we got the invite two months ago. As I recall, he said he was so looking forward to meeting all my little business chums. I just hope he behaves himself, particularly with the waiters."

Dominic recalled, somewhat fondly, their first visit to the Savoy River Room in London for dinner. Jonathan had behaved outrageously. As a result, they had got to know several of the diners really quite well and had received the best service from the waiters, all of whom Jonathan had flirted with throughout the night.

Dominic looked out at the front of the hospital. Samantha Gregory was now standing outside the main entrance with a cigarette in one hand and a handkerchief to her eyes. "Gillian, I have to go. Call me if anything urgent comes up." He ended the call and got out of the car.

As he walked to the hospital entrance, Samantha looked up, hastily stubbed out her cigarette, and dabbed her reddened eyes with the handkerchief. "I'm really not a smoker, Dominic," she said guiltily. "Or rather, I'm not any longer. But with everything that's happened, I'm afraid I've rather let myself go. Thank you so much for coming. You must be terribly busy. Shall we go and have a coffee?"

The brightly lit hospital cafeteria was warm and noisy. Dominic ordered cappuccinos for both of them, and they settled at a table in a quiet corner next to a poster showing the dangers of smoking.

"Rather appropriate and rather hideous, wouldn't you say?" commented Samantha, glancing at the image of smoke-damaged lungs. She twisted the handkerchief into a knot. "They say that Simon had a quiet night, and there's a tiny improvement in his kidneys. It gives one hope, of course."

"That's good. They'll always be cautious about unnecessarily raising your hopes, so it's a piece of good news," replied Dominic. "Have you found somewhere to stay?"

"Yes. It's really very pleasant—a little guesthouse not far from the seafront. In different circumstances it would be nice to be by the sea for a few days, even in December." She sighed. "Mr. Delingpole. Dominic. I'm not sure where to begin, but I would be grateful for your help. I have to speak to the police at two this afternoon, and I would like you to be with me. I will obviously pay you for your time."

"Mrs. Gregory, I would be very happy to have you as a client, but I'm not sure in what way I can act for you."

Samantha smiled as she said, "And neither am I just at the moment. Let's call you a professional friend. I have no one else who I can turn to, and your legal mind will help me to see things a little more clearly. As you can tell, I'm a little emotional just now." She turned away to wipe a tear from the corner of her eye. Then she looked at him steadily.

"Simon and I are very close. Ever since Richard, his father, died in a climbing accident, we have become a very tight family unit. I'd like to think Simon and I can tell each other everything."

Dominic wondered if she was keeping up a brave front, or whether she really believed Simon told her everything. Her comments clearly contradicted what Simon's housemate Jay had said an hour ago. Dominic decided that, as she was his client, he owed her the duty of honesty, and he should tell her about what he had learned in the last few hours.

"Samantha, I'm afraid I believe Simon may not have confided everything in you in recent times. I went to see John this morning before coming here. He told me about their relationship and how Simon was not yet ready to tell you."

Samantha smiled.

"Dominic, I'm his mother. Do you think I didn't know?" She sighed. "I knew he was finding it difficult to tell me, and I was waiting for him to pick the right time. I didn't want to rush him." She paused. "But yes, you're right, and I'm wrong. Simon hasn't confided everything to me. I merely know and I'm waiting for him to tell me. John's a lovely boy, and I was just pleased to know that Simon is happy."

Samantha narrowed her eyes slightly as she asked, "But why do you think that means he must have kept other secrets from me? Surely you of all people must know how difficult it is to come out?"

Dominic blushed briefly. "Everyone's circumstances are different, of course, and for young people it really is much easier...."

"Oh nonsense! Can I just say that I think it's a bit rich for you to judge Simon when you're so secretive about yourself? We spent nearly three hours in the car together last night, and I still don't know whether or not you have a boyfriend!"

This time Dominic's face turned crimson. "Samantha, could we just get back to—"

"Well, do you?"

Dominic sighed. "I think it's my turn to acknowledge that I'm wrong. Yes, I do have a partner, and no, I'm not very open about it. In this day and age, it probably is unnecessary for me to be quite so discreet. But after a while, it gets to be almost a habit."

Samantha giggled. "Oh, Dominic, how delightfully bashful you are! I imagine that it's rare you have a conversation like this with your clients."

Dominic smiled. "Samantha, I can tell you truthfully that I have never had a conversation like this with my clients. You must meet Jonathan some time. I think you two would get on like a house on fire."

7

THEY ARRIVED at Brighton's main police station shortly before two o'clock that afternoon. A policewoman ushered them into a cramped interview room, lit by a single flickering fluorescent light. Dominic could already feel a headache coming on, and he sipped at the plastic cup of water set before him.

After a few moments with only the buzzing of the failing light to listen to, a young, uniformed police officer and an even younger woman police officer entered the room.

"Mrs. Gregory?" asked the young police officer. "I'm Sergeant Dixon, and this is Constable Crawford." He turned to Dominic. "And you are?"

"This is my lawyer, Mr. Delingpole," replied Samantha briskly. "How can we help you, Sergeant?"

The young sergeant turned to look at Samantha. "We attended your son's house at 4:00 p.m. on Tuesday 9th December, following a call to the emergency services. Paramedics were already in attendance. Your son had apparently taken an overdose of a substance unknown and was unconscious. The paramedics reported that his breathing was shallow and his heart rate was significantly raised. Another resident of the house, John Fraser, was present. He confirmed that he had made the emergency call. Simon Gregory was transferred to the Royal Sussex Hospital, where he's currently being treated. I believe you've already seen him."

Sergeant Dixon paused and then said, "Mrs. Gregory, we've received the toxicology report on your son from the hospital. They've found significant traces of a recreational drug called ketamine or K. It may cause permanent damage to his kidneys and other organs. Were you aware that your son was regularly taking drugs?"

Dominic looked across at Samantha to see how she would react to the question. She took a sharp intake of breath. It was as though she had been hit with a fist. He resisted his instinct to reach out and take her hand.

"Sergeant, I don't believe my son takes drugs."

"Mrs. Gregory, the toxicology report is clear. We've a warrant to search the house, and officers are there now. Ketamine was reclassified as a class B drug because we now know it can be very dangerous." Sergeant Dixon's voice softened. "Mrs. Gregory, I'm very sorry. Often the parents are the last to know about what their children get up to once they get to university. I'm sorry you've had to find out this way. Does he live with you outside of term time?"

Before Samantha could reply, Dominic interjected, "Mr. Gregory is now living full-time in Brighton at that address. I would have preferred that you had notified Mrs. Gregory before searching her son's house. I trust you'll restore it to a good state afterwards?" As he said it, Dominic thought of the grubby, untidy house he had left this morning, and he was struck by the irony of his question.

"Mr. Delingpole, as I'm sure you know, we're not obliged to inform suspects' parents of our plans to—"

"Suspect?" asked Dominic sharply. "In precisely what way is Mr. Gregory a suspect?"

The sergeant sighed. "Mr. Gregory is suspected of possessing class B drugs, given the quantities of the substance showing in his body. We must now investigate whether he's in possession of any other illegal substances and in what quantities. That's the reason for the search."

"Will he be charged, Sergeant?" Samantha Gregory spoke quietly.

"I can't say at this stage of our investigations, Mrs. Gregory," replied Sergeant Dixon. "Obviously we're keen to interview him but, in his present condition—" He was interrupted as an officer entered the room. Yet again he appeared very young to Dominic, who was beginning to feel the generation gap acutely. He wondered idly if the British police force was now recruiting its officers directly from primary school. The pale-faced young officer passed a note to Sergeant Dixon, who studied it for a moment and then stood up.

"Mrs. Gregory, I'm afraid we need to get to the hospital as quickly as possible. Your son is all right, though still unconscious. But the hospital has reported an intruder was apprehended attempting to enter your son's room in the ICU."

"An intruder? What do you mean?" asked Samantha.

"An ICU nurse stopped a man who was about to enter the room. When she started to question him, he ran off."

"Perhaps he was just one of Simon's friends from university," said Samantha.

"I doubt it, Mrs. Gregory. Apparently in his haste to escape he dropped a hypodermic, containing enough ketamine to knock out a cavalry of horses. I'm afraid I think someone was trying to kill Simon."

DOMINIC TRIED to keep his Audi close behind the police car as he followed it through the outskirts of Brighton towards the hospital. Beside him, Samantha Gregory was triumphant.

"I told you he wasn't a druggie! I told you he didn't do that kind of thing. But why on earth would someone want to kill Simon? I can't imagine he mixes with the sorts of people who hire assassins to prowl hospital corridors."

Samantha stared out of the window as Dominic slowed the car to a halt at the crossing lights. A small group of people began to pass in front of them, and Dominic immediately noticed the unmistakable striding figure of his partner. He sounded the horn and wound down his window. "Jonathan! What are you doing here?"

Jonathan peeled off from the gaggle of pedestrians and loped over to the car. "Hello, lover boy! Who's your lady friend? Oh, you must be the famous Samantha. Hello my darling. Dominic has told me so much about you. Where are you off to?"

By this time the crossing had cleared, and cars behind Dominic were starting to sound their horns. Jonathan turned to look at the impatient drivers, waved, and then bowed.

"Jonathan, mind out of the way," said Dominic, embarrassed. "We've got to get to the hospital quickly. We're following that police car ahead, but you're holding us up."

"A police chase! How thrilling!" cried Jonathan. "Then I shall definitely ride with you." Ignoring Dominic's protests, he ran around to the passenger door and opened it, saying, "My dear Samantha! I am Dominic's friend and lover, Jonathan McFadden. Would you mind awfully letting me squeeze into the back of Diana? I presume Dominic told you that's what I christened this heavenly car."

The drivers in the cars behind them were now growing angrier, and the sounds of the horns got more insistent. Jonathan made one final bow to the furious motorists, kissed Samantha full on the lips, and then dived onto the backseat.

"I'm very pleased to meet you at last, Mr. McFadden," said Samantha. "Dominic has said so little about you."

Dominic blushed in the seat next to her. He flashed his lights at the police car ahead of him, which had pulled over to the side of the road, hoping he would not have to explain why he was stopping to pick up passengers while under police escort to the hospital.

"Yes, dear Dominic is very coy. I love him dearly but I can't for the life of me understand why our relationship has to be kept under the cloak of invisibility."

"In case you've forgotten, I'm still here, Jonathan," said Dominic irritably.

"I know, lover, which is precisely why I'm saying this to the charming Samantha. Now, what news of your son, dear?"

Samantha half turned in her seat to talk to Jonathan. "It's terrible. The reason we're on the way to the hospital now is that the police believe someone was trying to kill him."

"Murder! So he didn't take an overdose. It's terrible, but you must be relieved that it wasn't an attempt by his own hand. What makes them suspect murder?"

Samantha explained the new development to Jonathan

as Dominic turned into the hospital car park and found a space. Together, they walked across to the main entrance, where an impatient Sergeant Dixon was waiting.

"I thought you were following us," he said crossly. Dominic felt his face flush. "And who's this?" asked the officer, turning to Jonathan.

"I am Mrs. Gregory's advisor, Jonathan McFadden," said Jonathan before Dominic had a chance to speak. "She's invited me to be with her this afternoon. Do carry on, Officer."

Sergeant Dixon eyed Jonathan suspiciously before saying, "It seems that we may have an image of the suspect on the hospital closed-circuit television. We'd like you to come and see if you can identify him, Mrs. Gregory."

He led the way down a flight of stairs to the hospital security office. Ranged along the left-hand wall of the office was a bank of monitors showing images that periodically switched to show views of the car park, main entrance, corridors, and the wards.

Sitting in front of the monitors was a well-built security guard with close-cropped hair. His short-sleeved white shirt revealed some highly developed pectoral muscles and his passion for tattoos.

"Goodness me, you seem to have cameras everywhere," said Jonathan. "There's no escaping Big Brother, now, is there?" Jonathan's eyes were glued to the security guard's torso.

The guard turned his eyes from the monitors to look at Jonathan. "We get all sorts coming into the hospital," he said, his eyes slowly scanning Jonathan's body. "You won't believe what people get up to, even when they know there's a camera watching them." The man spoke with a strong

French accent. Dominic hoped he would say some more. It was very seductive.

"Maybe people get up to all sorts because they know there's a camera watching them," said Jonathan with a wink.

Sergeant Dixon stepped forward. "We're here to look at the ICU recordings from earlier today," he said frostily. "Could you set them up for Mrs. Gregory to view, please?"

The security guard turned his eyes away from Jonathan and began punching a series of buttons on his console. "Is this the patient's relative? I've got the suspected intruder on several cameras, actually. But the best face shot is when he first arrives in reception. Let me just enhance it for you."

The slightly fuzzy image of a dark-haired man around thirty years old sharpened on the large screen on the security guard's console. The man was staring almost straight at the camera.

"We put the camera next to the main signage in reception. That way when people look at the signs to find out where to go, we get a clear view of their faces on the security cameras," said the guard proudly.

"Mrs. Gregory, do you recognize the man at all?" asked Sergeant Dixon.

Samantha shook her head. Dominic stared at the image frozen on the screen of the man who was apparently on his way to try to kill Samantha's son. Then he turned to look at Jonathan, who was also staring at the screen. He looked like he had just seen a ghost.

Jonathan glanced at Dominic and shook his head. Dominic turned to Sergeant Dixon and said, "What happens now?"

"Well, there'll be an officer permanently posted outside Mr. Gregory's door, and we'll attempt a match of the face against our database. We'll show the image to Simon's housemates and see if we get a positive identification," replied Sergeant Dixon.

Jonathan seemed to have recovered from whatever had shaken him up a minute earlier. "What about fingerprints on the hypodermic?" he asked. Dominic rolled his eyes. He knew his partner's passion for watching *CSI* too well. He preferred a gentle episode of *Miss Marple* any day.

"We'll check, but I imagine he'd be wearing latex gloves. After all, there's a ready supply in a hospital. Right, I think we're finished here. Mrs. Gregory, do you have some form of photo ID with you? You'll need to show it to the officer on duty whenever you go to see your son. Would you like anyone else to be allowed access?"

Samantha looked thoughtful for a moment. "This business has really shaken me up. I'm not sure that I'd like anyone else to go in while he remains unconscious."

"What about John?" asked Dominic. "They seem very close."

Samantha's voice hardened as she turned to Dominic. "You know, I've never met the boy before I came here, and Simon never mentioned him to me. He can sit in with me if he likes, but after what's happened today, I'm not taking any chances with Simon's life." She turned to Sergeant Dixon. "I want my son to live. You will allow no visitor into his room except the medical staff and me. His life is in your hands, officer."

They left the security office, Jonathan casting one last admiring glance at the security guard's rippling shirt. As they filed up the staircase to the hospital reception area, Dominic pulled Jonathan back.

"Tell me. You saw something in there. What was it?"

"Those tattoos on his arms. They were just heavenly."

Dominic squeezed Jonathan's arm tighter. "On the screen, idiot. You recognized him, didn't you?"

Jonathan smiled benignly. "I thought I'd seen the face somewhere before, but then I wasn't so sure. It could have been in any number of bars. That's why I didn't want to say anything to that dreary police officer. It would lead to all sorts of awkward questions about where I spend some of my nights."

"But if you told them, you could be helping the police find whoever tried to kill Samantha's son," protested Dominic.

"And I will," said Jonathan. "Christophe and I are going on a little cruise tonight to see if we can find him. Do you want to come? You might have some fun and knock some of that lawyer stuffiness out of you."

Dominic bristled. Jonathan could be infuriating at times. He knew that he still cruised the gay bars of Brighton and London on a few occasions, despite their two-year relationship. Jonathan had made it plain from the start that he wanted the freedom to go on the occasional cruise when Dominic was not around. Dominic had agreed, mainly because there was little he could do to stop Jonathan, and also because it gave him a frisson of excitement to think that, even after encounters with the young men of Brighton and London, Jonathan still chose to share his life with Dominic. Then again, he still felt the occasional twinge of jealousy.

Dominic glowered at Jonathan. "Who's Christophe?"

"He's the possessor of those rather fine tattoos that we just met. Very French. And I know you're a sucker for a French accent."

"I didn't hear you organize anything with him, and we weren't introduced to him. When did all this happen, and how do you know his name's Christophe?" demanded Dominic.

"Name badge on his shirt, dear thing. Surely you noticed that?" retorted Jonathan, a shade defensively. "I haven't organized anything yet, but I'm very confident he'd welcome a night out with me. And you for that matter," he added hastily.

Before Dominic could say anything more, Jonathan disappeared back down the stairs to arrange his nocturnal rendezvous, leaving Dominic wondering whether he was beginning to get out of his depth. He was now aware of two pieces of evidence that had been withheld from the police. First by John and now by Jonathan. As a lawyer he felt awkward, knowing that there were potentially tough penalties for obstructing the police. But his loyalty to Jonathan and his compassion for John led him to decide that, for the moment at least, he would not be approaching Sergeant Dixon.

Jonathan's smiling face reappeared at the foot of the stairs a moment later. "Such a nice boy is young Christophe," he said jauntily, bounding up the stairs. "He's printing off several copies of the face from the security camera and will be pleased to join us around ten tonight when he's finished his shift. We'll meet at Legends and then go on from there. Could be a fun night, and profitable for you and our dear Samantha. Winners all round."

8

LEGENDS WAS Dominic's idea of hell. A brash gay hotel on Brighton's seafront just east of the main pier, it housed an in-your-face restaurant and bar open most hours of the day and night. The clientele spent their time either eyeing each other up and down, or watching their own reflections in the myriad mirrors around the brightly lit cocktail bar. Music pumped out on all sides, and Dominic was jostled by muscle Marys and boisterous bears as he followed Jonathan to the bar that evening.

He knew this was just one of Jonathan's several haunts in Brighton, and as he surveyed the male meat market around him, he wondered how their relationship could possibly stay intact with Jonathan coming to places like this from time to time. Dominic felt awkward and exposed, whereas clearly Jonathan was at home here. It took them some time to reach the bar as Jonathan stopped to embrace and kiss men he encountered on the way. Dominic trailed behind, feeling like some kind of equerry following a minor royal. He smiled politely at the beautiful young things who eyed him curiously, some even scornfully.

Standing at the bar was the security guard from the hospital. He had changed his short-sleeved work shirt for a T-shirt that highlighted his hours of hard work in the gym all the more. Dominic had to admit Christophe had a very attractive body, and one that could not be recreated simply by taking bracing walks in the Chiltern Hills.

Jonathan bought Corona beers for him and Christophe, and a bright blue non-alcoholic cocktail for Dominic. Jonathan had volunteered him as the driver for that evening. They moved to the end of the bar, and Christophe produced a cardboard folder containing prints of the face in the security image they had seen in his control room earlier.

"You know," he said with his strong French accent, "I think that I have seen him before as well. It was in a bar in Brighton, I think, but not this one. Or maybe it was the club downstairs. It was dark, anyway."

They all stared at the image for a moment. Despite enhancement it was not in sharp focus, and it was particularly difficult to see the man's eyes clearly. He had short dark hair, almost completely covered by the hood of the sweatshirt he was wearing. His forehead was large, balanced by a nose that was equally large set above a small, tight-lipped mouth. In the photo they could see he was carrying what seemed to be a pair of surgical gloves and a small plastic bag.

Dominic looked around the packed bar. Was this face somewhere in here? It was difficult to tell because of the poor quality of the frozen image. As his gaze flicked from one face to another, he realized that those he was staring at were regarding him with equal fascination. All at once he felt embarrassed and looked down at his beer.

Jonathan shouted in his ear, "What's the matter? Not enjoying being eye candy for the good folk of Brighton?"

Dominic flushed and looked up at Jonathan's smiling face. He decided to keep his comments to the business in hand.

"When you first saw that face on the video screen, you went as white as a sheet," said Dominic. "Why aren't you so certain now?"

"I don't know, really," replied Jonathan. "Except when we first saw the image, it was moving—before Christophe froze it on the screen. I think it must have been something to do with the way he was moving on the video." Jonathan's eyes lit up and he looked across at Christophe excitedly. "That's it! Do you remember the way he walked just before he stopped and you got this freeze-frame?"

Christophe was already nodding. "Yes, I do now. He looked as if he had a bad leg. He looked as if he was not walking correctly."

"He had a limp!" shouted Jonathan across the Legends noise. "And now I remember where I've seen him before. It wasn't here or in any club in fact."

"Do you mean there was no need to come to this godforsaken place tonight after all?" shouted Dominic crossly. "We could have spent a pleasant evening in the Slug and Lettuce instead."

Jonathan turned his piercing blue eyes on Dominic. "Oh, my dear thing, is this not fun for you? We can go somewhere much quieter now if you like. It's the place where I'm damn certain I've seen this reprobate before."

Dominic suddenly had a sinking feeling as he asked, "And where would that be?"

"Why, the sauna of course! It's only a short walk down the seafront to Old Steine. It'll do you the world of good, and you could get a massage to loosen up those tense shoulders of yours if you like."

Dominic sighed. If Legends was his idea of hell, then a gay sauna bath was, for him, a level below hell. There was something about strutting about in a steamy atmosphere on slippery tiles with a towel wrapped around his waist that filled him with dread. He was convinced that all saunas were infected with Legionnaire's disease, to add further to his misery. He turned to Jonathan to make his excuses and duck out, but Jonathan had already finished his bottle of beer and was talking excitedly into the ear of a barman wearing a black singlet. After a few moments, he handed the barman one of the photographs and scrawled his phone number on the back of it. The barman laughed, revealing a brilliant set of perfectly white teeth, and then kissed Jonathan on both cheeks.

As they walked out of the bar, now even fuller than when they had entered, Dominic shouted into Jonathan's ear, "That's the most unusual chat-up line I've yet seen you use. Can't we just hand this over to the police now?" But Jonathan just smiled serenely and led Dominic and Christophe out into the damp night air.

THE SAUNA was a few minutes' walk from Legends Hotel. Buffeted by the December wind, Dominic was feeling the cold and tried again to make his excuses and leave. "I really think this is a matter for the police now, Jonathan. You have important information for them, and it's not for us to be playing Starsky and Hutch—"

"I rather fancy us as Cagney and Lacey, actually," interrupted Jonathan mischievously. He stopped and turned to look at Dominic. "Anyway, I think you're right. I can't imagine what we would do if the bad guy turns out to be in there. It's going to be difficult making a citizen's arrest when I'm wearing nothing but a smile. We'll get a taxi from the rank in Old Steine and go over to the police station to meet the sweet young detective and his girlfriend."

The three men walked past the entrance to the sauna. As they did so, the door opened, and a man pushed past them, heading down towards the seafront. Christophe suddenly shouted, "De Dieu! C'est lui. Jonathan. That's him."

Dominic glanced over his shoulder and saw the man, alerted by Christophe's shout no doubt, turn to look at them. He hesitated for a moment before turning and running towards the main traffic junction, his left leg slightly dragging as if stiff and inflexible.

Christophe sprinted off first, followed by Jonathan and then Dominic. Despite having a head start, the man's left leg was slowing him down, and it would take just a few more seconds for Christophe to catch up with him.

The traffic lights at the junction had just changed as the fleeing man ran into the path of a black Range Rover. His body flew up into the air and landed on the windscreen. The car screeched to a halt as the body slid off the car and onto the road. Dominic was already reaching for his mobile phone as Christophe and then Jonathan got to the intersection. The driver's door of the Range Rover slowly heaved open, and a tall, well-built young man climbed out of the car.

"He ran in front of me. There was nothing I could do." The young man repeated the phrase several times over. He held his baldhead in his hands for a moment before looking up at the three men. "Didn't you see? He ran out in front of me. I had no chance. I'll call an ambulance."

He pulled out his phone, and a few moments later he was describing the location to the person at the other end of the phone. Dominic noticed the man had a small tattoo of an eagle on his neck. The man finished his call and turned to the others.

"The ambulance will be here shortly," he announced.

Christophe was examining the body on the ground.

"I will not move him until the ambulance gets here," he said. "But I do not think he is alive."

The driver looked across to Christophe. "Are you certain?" he asked. Christophe nodded.

Jonathan took Dominic's arm and pulled him out of earshot of the driver of the Range Rover. "I'll leave you to do the talking when the boys in blue arrive," he said grimly. "You're the lawyer. But before they arrive, what should Christophe do with that folder of photographs?"

Dominic was furious with himself for being so stupid. Why had he allowed Jonathan to seduce him into this ridiculous adventure? It might have felt like a bit of fun to start with, but it had ended in an unnecessary death for which they were at least partly responsible. Even worse, for all they knew, the body of the man on the road might not be that of Simon's attempted murderer, but that of an innocent man, terrified of being discovered leaving a gay sauna and chased by three men he had never seen before.

"This is serious, Jonathan. We must tell the police everything we know and let them do their job. We can't play amateur detectives any longer."

By this time the driver of the black Range Rover was back on his mobile phone, talking about what had happened. Dominic walked across to Christophe where he crouched beside the body on the road and bent down to take a closer look. The man was probably no more than thirty years old, wearing a heavy winter coat and scarf and what appeared to be a smart navy suit underneath. A much more sophisticated style than the jeans and hoodie he had been wearing in the hospital. Dominic took a close look at the man's face. There was no doubt; it was the face they had seen on the security monitor. Who was he and why had he apparently been intent on killing Simon Gregory? Dominic stood up and went to lean heavily against the back of the car as a wave of nausea threatened to overwhelm him. As he did so, Christophe reached inside the man's coat and pulled out a slim wallet.

"What the hell are you doing?" hissed Dominic to Christophe, not wanting to attract the attention of the car driver.

"You want to know who he is, don't you?" replied Christophe in a matter-of-fact tone. He pulled out the few cards that were in the wallet. "Here is his drivers' licence. It says his name is Peter Freedman, and he lives in Stockwell in London. He has another card here. For the House of Commons. Does this mean he is a Member of Parliament?" Christophe looked up at Dominic and handed him the card.

Dominic examined the photo identity card bearing the parliamentary crest. "No, this looks like a temporary pass that could be used by anyone who's working there. He could be a researcher, or he could be a cleaner, although judging by that suit and overcoat, I'd say he's not a cleaner. Is there anything else?" Dominic was now intrigued to know just who the man was and had set aside his initial qualms about Christophe's actions.

"There are a few credit cards and some money, but nothing else. No business cards." Christophe fumbled with the wallet. "There is a phone number here. No name, just the initials BK. I'll check the other pockets."

Christophe reached back inside the man's coat, but at that moment they heard the sound of sirens and saw the reflection of blue lights in the distance. Hastily, he put the wallet back and stood up as an ambulance turned into the street. A few moments later, it screeched to a halt alongside the body, and three men in green scrubs jumped out.

Dominic wished he were tucked up in his bed back in Oxfordshire. This was going to be a long night.

9

THE THREE students sat around the kitchen table. It was an emergency house meeting to discuss the aftermath of the police search a few hours earlier. Not much was being said and there were a lot of silences. They all felt numb with shock after witnessing all their possessions turned inside out by the forensics team.

Gemma broke the silence first. "They even cut open my teddy bear. How shitty is that? What do they think I am? Some kind of drugs mule?"

Jay was flipping a beer mat on the edge of the table. "Do you think we can claim compensation or something? They've fucking destroyed my room, even ripped the carpet up. Then they just walk out and leave us with this shit to clear up. It's not as if they found anything."

John looked up at him. "How can you be so sure? They took a lot of plastic evidence bags away with them. Who knows what they found in Si's room? And what about your stuff from Barton Kane?"

Jay rounded on John. "Shit, you're damn quick to bring that up every time, aren't you? I'm not dumb enough to keep it here, am I? Anyway, there was no stuff in Si's room. I cleared it before they got here."

John was seething as he stood up. "You went into Si's room and went through his stuff? You little shit!"

"What the fuck else did you think I'd do? I didn't want the police finding something and trying to pin it on us. You should be grateful I did. He had some pretty weird porn shit in a rucksack under the bed. I took that out before they arrived."

John crossed the kitchen and stood over Jay. "Who the hell do you think you are, taking Si's stuff from his room? Where did you put it?"

Jay stood up, his face inches away from John's. "Wouldn't you like to know, lover boy? I got it out of the house, of course. It's in the skip across the street. I reckoned they wouldn't go through that. At least, I hoped they wouldn't. Go and dig it out now if you need to. Did you know he was into bondage and shit?" Jay's pearly white teeth gleamed as his face broke into a wide smile. "So that's what you two faggots were up to, was it? Christ, you're one hell of a piece of work."

John's face flushed. He was hearing about a side of Simon he knew nothing about, and he was hearing it from Jay of all people.

"It's none of your damn business, but no, that's not 'our thing' at all."

John stormed out of the kitchen and walked outside to the skip that had been sitting across the road from their house ever since they had moved in. Under the orange glow of the streetlamp, he started rummaging through a mound of builders' rubbish. A few minutes later, Jay appeared on the path, with Gemma just behind him.

"Look, mate, I'm sorry," said Jay. "I've got a mouth and no brain, and this whole thing is freaking me out right now. I know it's really shitty for you because of you and Simon being—" He searched for the words. "—for being so close. Look, it's a scruffy rucksack you need to find. I put it in a supermarket bag before I shoved it in there so it would be less conspicuous. It should be somewhere here." With that, he started digging around in one end of the skip. A few moments later, he pulled out a grubby, damp white-and-blue plastic supermarket bag and handed it to John. "Here you go, mate. It's all yours. None of my business."

John took the bag and pulled out the large black rucksack. He turned it over in his hands and examined it curiously. "I've not seen Simon with this before, but then, I suppose I don't know everything about him," he said in a flat voice. "I'm going to take a look at it back in the house. If he's hiding stuff from me, maybe it's none of my business either. But this whole thing has got out of control. There might be something in here to explain what's happened in the last few days."

As John walked back into the house, Jay looked over at Gemma.

"All right now?" he asked.

She stared at John's receding figure. "It wasn't just porn, was it?" she said quietly. "What else was in there that made you hide it? Were there drugs as well?"

Jay rubbed his face nervously. "Not much escapes you, missy, does it?" He paused. "There was some really weird porn, but there was something else that I didn't think would do Simon any good if the police got hold of it. We'd better go inside. John's about to get a bit of a shock about his beloved Simon."

SAMANTHA SAT staring at the unconscious figure of her son, her mind whirling with all that had happened in such a short space of time. She was desperate for sleep, but since returning from the security office, she had not wanted to leave him in case something happened while she was away. For her, the police officer posted outside the door of Simon's intensive care room was not enough. Her protective motherly instincts kept her at her son's bedside.

A nurse had offered her the small bed at the end of the ward, normally used by the staff, but Samantha had refused, preferring to doze fitfully in the chair. Seeing the security images of the hooded figure earlier had made her angry and frightened in equal measure. She had also begun to wonder what secrets her son had been keeping from her. The fact that he had not been open about his sexuality was, as far as she was concerned, entirely understandable. But she feared that there were other secrets he had withheld, otherwise why would someone try to kill him? Whoever the killer was, they had made two attempts now, and they were desperate enough to risk entering the hospital a second time. Samantha had so many questions. Sitting next to Simon, listening to the insistent beeps of the monitoring equipment, she felt alone.

From across the room, her phone buzzed as a new message arrived. The nursing staff had told her she could keep her mobile switched on provided she kept it at a safe distance from the monitors. She got up and walked over to check the screen. It was from John. The fourth text in an hour. The previous three had been asking her why he could not visit Simon. The wording of John's messages was increasingly desperate. They asked after Simon's condition and whether or not he was getting any worse.

But this latest text was different. In it John claimed he

had something important for her to know. That he needed to talk to her. Samantha put the phone down and went back to sit at her son's bedside. Perhaps she was being too hard on John. But with the recent turn of events, she felt she could no longer trust anyone. She did not want to leave Simon's bedside, and she did not want anyone else in the room, even if she was there in person.

The phone buzzed again. Wearily, Samantha hauled herself out of the rigid plastic chair and went over to look at the screen again. At that moment, the sounds from the monitoring equipment changed. The beeping rate increased, and an alarm sounded. Samantha whirled around, panic-struck that her mobile had triggered something with the sensitive equipment.

The door burst open as a nurse hurried into the room.

"I'm so sorry," Samantha began, but the nurse ignored her and went to the trolley of electronics by the side of the bed. Samantha looked across at Simon. Was it her imagination, or did his face twitch? She rushed to his side and held his hand in hers, staring intently at his face. There it was again! His left eyebrow twitched, and the side of his mouth moved slightly around the ventilator tube inserted down his throat.

"Nurse," she half whispered, "he's moving!"

"Yes, I know," said the nurse as she reset an alarm on one of the instruments. "It can be quite common for patients in comas to demonstrate involuntary facial muscle spasms sometimes. Don't read too much into it just yet. Although there does seem to have been a change to his respiration and heart rate in the last minute or so. That's why the alarm went off."

Simon's hand momentarily tightened under Samantha's,

then relaxed again. At the same time, his head stirred on the pillow.

"I'll go and get the registrar," said the nurse. "I think young Simon may be coming back to us." She hurriedly left the room.

Samantha's own heartbeat quickened, and she grasped Simon's hand tightly in her own. There was no way she was leaving him now. John's text messages would just have to go unanswered.

10

AT JUST before midnight, Dominic, Jonathan, and Christophe sat at the bar of the Bulldog pub in St. James's Street, the main road that snaked through Kemp Town, the gay district on the eastern end of Brighton. For Dominic it was mercifully quiet, with no thumping music like the brightly lit and pulsating Legends. It had been Jonathan's suggestion to retreat to the oldest gay pub in Brighton. Partly because they all needed a drink, and partly because it had recently become fashionable with gay students in the city. He suggested it might be an opportunity to find out if Simon had ever visited there.

Dominic was not feeling good. The phrase "economical with the truth" kept echoing in his head. The police had questioned them at the scene of the accident, and he had provided most of the answers. He had truthfully told them that they had witnessed the accident after leaving the sauna. What he had not told them was that they had been chasing the man. True, the police had not asked any questions as to why they thought the man had run into the path of the black Range Rover. But he had not volunteered the information either, and he felt uncomfortable with that. It was one thing not to volunteer information in his legal disputes for clients. It was quite another to withhold key information from the police.

The police were more concerned about dealing with the dead body and the driver, so the three men had not been kept long at the roadside. They were invited to visit the police station the following day to give witness statements and to answer more questions. It was this invitation that they were talking about at the bar, the discussion occasionally interrupted by Jonathan and Christophe breaking off to stare when yet another beautiful young thing arrived late in the bar. Dominic was in the middle of his latest proposal for handling the situation when Christophe and Jonathan again turned their heads to eye two young men who had just entered the bar. Exasperated, Dominic picked up his drink and took a long draft of his lemonade. He longed to get back to Jonathan's cottage so he could pour himself a straight malt whiskey and finally unwind from the evening.

Dominic turned to see what latest "talent" his drinking companions were ogling and nearly dropped his drink in his lap. Standing at the entrance were two young men. One he had not seen before, but the other was John from the student house.

He grabbed Jonathan's shoulder and pulled him close to say in his ear, "That's the boy! That's Simon's friend, John. I wonder who he's with." Dominic shifted so that Jonathan and Christophe masked him from John's view. He did not want to scare John away before he had properly settled in the club, and he certainly did not want another chase like the one earlier that evening.

"What are you doing?" asked Jonathan. "Don't you want him to see you? Why don't you nip through to the toilet? It's just behind us. Happy to start up a little chat with him. He's very cute, and so is his friend. You can pop back in a short while once he's sat down at my side."

Feeling unnecessarily furtive, Dominic slipped behind Jonathan and through the toilet door. It was a move he instantly regretted. Hanging around pub toilets was not his scene and never had been. He tried to go into one of the two cubicles, but they were both occupied. He started to wash his hands and became aware of a man around his age wearing jeans that were far too tight and a fake biker's jacket. The man was staring at him in the mirror. Dominic turned away to the hand dryer to find it was broken. He looked around for paper towels to find the dispenser empty.

"It's such a bore, isn't it?" said the man, suddenly at his side. Dominic backed away, shaking his hands in a vain attempt to dry them. He was far too tired to be polite to the unattractive pickup. He just wanted to walk out, but it was too soon for him to re-join Jonathan at the bar.

"Well, if you're not interested, then why the fuck did you follow me in here?" said the man with a pained expression on his face. Before Dominic could protest, the man had stormed out the door. Dominic sighed. Judging by the sounds emanating from both the cubicles, they were occupied with men engaged in activities other than evacuating their bowels. He felt like he was watching a porn movie wearing a blindfold. An activity that he was confident he would never try.

MEANWHILE, JONATHAN had latched on to John and his companion when they approached the bar.

"Hello, boys. It's a bit late for twinks like you to be up,

isn't it? Can I get you an ice cream soda, or would you prefer something stronger?"

John looked acutely embarrassed, but his friend was much more eager to play along. He turned to John and said loudly, "I know you said you preferred older men, but cocoa drinkers should really stick by the fireside with their slippers on a night like this."

To which Jonathan promptly retorted, "Horlicks I'm not into, but we can explore other kinds of licks later. I'm Jonathan and this is Christophe. Beer or a short?"

The young man laughed and replied, "I'm Steve, and this is John. Corona if you're buying. We skipped shorts tonight." His dark brown puppy eyes flashed at Jonathan as he added, "But maybe later."

As Jonathan was ordering the drinks, he took the opportunity to eye up John's companion. His youthful looks were deceptive. He seemed quite a bit older than John. Probably in his late twenties, if not early thirties. His head was shaved, and his athletic body sported a polo top and tight-legged jeans with braces and a pair of 14-hole Grinder boots on his feet. He looked a world apart from the sensitive-looking, Byronesque John.

"So, are you two boys together?" asked Christophe, closely eyeing Steve as Jonathan handed out the drinks.

"Oh no. John's spoken for and couldn't possibly sully himself with trade like me." John's face flushed red, but Steve just grinned as he went on, "Let's just say we do a little business together sometimes. I help John out when he's in need." John's face turned a shade darker.

"Hello, John," said a voice behind them. "What sort of business would that be, then?"

DOMINIC WAS rather proud of his dramatic entrance. It certainly had an immediate effect on John, who shrank visibly.

"Mr. Delingpole, hi,'" he mumbled. "I didn't expect to see you here."

"Clearly," said Dominic brusquely. "So tell me, John, exactly what business do you do outside your studies with this young man?"

"What's it to you, mate?" asked Steve harshly. "Are you the police or something?"

"God no, we're not the police," cut in Jonathan quickly. "This is my partner and lover, Dominic Delingpole. He's a lawyer and finds it a bit hard to switch off sometimes. Look, let's get a round of drinks going. Money please, Dominic."

Dominic glowered at Jonathan and pulled his wallet out of his back pocket. Deflated after his theatrical arrival, he realized that perhaps he had been a little heavy-handed and grudgingly admired Jonathan's deft gear change. All the same he would like to know just what business John and Steve were involved in.

"Dominic tells me you share a house with the boy in the hospital," Jonathan began. "Did you know someone tried to kill him today?"

John's hand jumped as he reached for his drink, knocking the glass and spilling its contents over Dominic's sleeve.

"Oh my God," said John, turning to Dominic. "Why didn't anyone tell me? Shit. Is that why they won't let me see him? Mr. Delingpole, why didn't you tell me? You know how much he means...." John's voice faltered.

"To be honest I thought that the police would be wanting to talk to you about it," replied Dominic. "It's pretty obvious now that someone wants Simon dead. Can you think who his enemies are? They're very determined. You know him better than any of us here, John, and certainly better than his mother. I offered to help her, that's what I'm going to do. And I think it's time you did too. Just who's he been mixing with that would twice try to kill him?"

Dominic stared hard at John's face as he spoke. He wondered if the young man knew more than he was revealing. All he could see was bewilderment and fear. John said nothing, absent-mindedly mopping up his spilled drink with a bar towel. It was Steve who spoke first.

"Come on, mate. Grandpa here's right. After what you discovered tonight, don't you think it's time to tell them about your suspicions about not-so-innocent Simon?"

Dominic settled back on the wire-framed barstool, relieved that they might finally be getting somewhere. At that moment his phone rang.

11

———

SAMANTHA STOOD by the vending machine, waiting for the sludgy brown liquid to stop pouring into the thin plastic cup. It was two in the morning, but she was wide-awake. Her mind was turning over and over the fragments of information she had been collecting.

After feeling Simon's hand tighten around her own, she was light-headed and elated. It seemed that her son was coming out of his coma. That it would only be a short time before he was fully conscious and she would be able to speak to him again.

Her optimism was short-lived. A young woman doctor walked past the door shortly after the nurse had left. Samantha knew that Simon wasn't the doctor's patient, but asked her advice anyway. The doctor politely confirmed what the nurse had told Samantha. Coma patients do sometimes move as though they are awake. She explained how some patients even make noises and get agitated. The movements that Simon was making did not mean he was coming out of his coma. The medical team needed to see other signs to be certain of that.

The young woman doctor appeared not much older than Simon, with an accent that Samantha guessed to be from somewhere in Eastern Europe or perhaps Russia. She had been very kind and understanding with Samantha but also very firm.

"You can't stay here with him all night. You are not helping him, and you're not helping yourself," the young woman had said before smiling and adding, "We don't want to have to admit you to the hospital as well for exhaustion. You must be strong for your son." Samantha had relented, which was how she came to be standing by the machine. Waiting for her hot brown beverage masquerading as coffee. She was in the almost-deserted reception lobby of the hospital, waiting for a minicab to turn up.

The taxi firm's business card was shoved into the frame of the vending machine. She had called them over twenty minutes ago. Frustrated with the wait, she called them again and listened to the insistent ringing as she sipped her ersatz coffee. After several minutes without an answer, the call disconnected. Samantha leaned against the glass windows of the reception area, her head swimming with the effects of the caffeine and exhaustion. She rested her eyes for a moment, desperately needing sleep. With her eyes still closed, she felt her way around the keypad of the aging mobile phone to redial the minicab company. She held the phone to her ear and listened to the ringing tone. Suddenly it was interrupted as a man's voice answered at the other end.

"Mrs. Gregory? Are you all right?" It was Dominic.

Samantha jerked upright, her eyes wide open, suddenly very awake.

"Dominic! Oh, I'm so sorry. I must have pressed the

wrong buttons on this phone. I really didn't mean to call you at this ungodly hour. I'm so sorry to have woken you up."

"Don't worry, Mrs. Gregory" came the weary voice from the other end. "I'm still very much awake, although I'd prefer to be in my bed just now."

Samantha listened intently to the sounds coming from the earpiece. "Is that music I can hear in the background, Dominic? Are you in a club somewhere? You're a man full of surprises, I must say."

"It's a long story, Mrs. Gregory—Samantha. I'll explain when I next see you. You're not still at the hospital, are you?"

"Actually, Dominic, I am, and as you're up and about, I wonder if you might help me? I've been trying to get a minicab to pick me up from here for the past half hour without success. Do you think you could find one other than ABC Taxis, who seem to be quite useless? If they could come to the hospital and pick me up and take me back to the guesthouse, I'd be so grateful. I desperately need some sleep, and Simon's medical team have finally persuaded me that I'm simply in the way here."

"I can do better than that, Samantha," said Dominic. "I can come and collect you myself. I was nominated to be the driver for this evening, so I have my car here."

Samantha began to protest, but Dominic interrupted. "Don't go away. I'll be there in fifteen minutes." He hung up, leaving Samantha much relieved.

———

DOMINIC TURNED to Jonathan who was leaning on the bar. "You find out what these young men have to say for themselves. Don't get distracted," he added, as Steve turned his back on them to talk to Christophe and Jonathan started to eye his rear admiringly. "I'll come straight back after I've dropped Samantha at her guesthouse."

Jonathan whispered in his ear, "My dear, there are so many ways of extracting information. If it involves a little flirting, don't be alarmed. I still love you more than dearly," and he extended his tongue into Dominic's ear briefly before giving him an affectionate kiss good-bye on the lips.

Dominic sighed as he walked out of the club. He wished that he could be as relaxed with his sexuality as Jonathan. Be less possessive when they were in company. He felt constrained by the conventions with which he had been brought up. Meeting Jonathan had been a breath of fresh air, what with his constant challenges to Dominic's ascetic approach to life. Being challenged was good for him, but also, well, challenging.

John asked to go with him to pick up Samantha, but Dominic pointed out that at this hour of the morning, all she wanted was sleep, not an emotional discussion about Simon's condition.

———

SAMANTHA CLIMBED into the front seat of Dominic's car. She gave him the address for her guesthouse before planting a grateful peck on his cheek. "My knight riding his silver charger," she sighed.

Dominic blushed and attempted to adopt a matter-of-fact tone as he asked, "Is there any change in Simon's condition?" He slipped the car into drive and pulled away as Samantha told him of the evening's developments in the ICU at the hospital.

"I really don't know what to think now," she said. "I'm sure that he was squeezing my hand, but they said it could be just involuntary movements. Perhaps I'm just wishing a bit too hard." She sighed and stared out of the window as they drove down the seafront road to her guesthouse. "Have you had a nice evening? It sounded like you were somewhere very noisy when I called you."

Dominic decided it was far too late to begin telling her of the evening's events. "Oh, it was yet another club Jonathan wanted to go to. Not as noisy as the first one we were in, but still, the music was not really my thing, I'm afraid. Jonathan thinks I'm a real stuffed shirt because of that. But I simply don't have his eclectic tastes in music. He loves so much—from Dvorak to Drum 'n' Bass. We only really overlap on classical, and then he knows so much more than me. His knowledge of classical music is astonishing. His mind is like a *Groves Dictionary*."

As they turned right into a quiet crescent of Victorian guesthouses, his mobile beeped with a new message. He brought the car to a halt by the side of the road, picked up the phone and saw that the message was from Jonathan:

Dramatic revelations. Hurry back lover. xx

"Is that Jonathan wanting to know where you are?" asked Samantha, unbuckling her seat belt. "You'll have to keep secret the wild, passionate love we had on the cramped backseat of your swanky car, won't you?" She turned, laid a hand on his knee, and kissed Dominic gently on the lips. "You're such a lovely man. Jonathan's very lucky."

She fumbled for the door handle.

"Forgive me. I'm very tired, and that was probably entirely inappropriate. Hurry back to him and don't let him go. You two are very fortunate." Samantha slipped out of the car and was gone.

Dominic slumped back in his seat, bemused and flattered in almost equal measure. He felt like the awkward teenager he had once been, both embarrassed and confused by girls who threw themselves at him and for whom he could not reciprocate with honesty. The strain had been almost intolerable in those days, and yet there had been no one to talk to about how he felt. He had gone through his first two years at Birmingham University with his head buried in his studies. He avoided potential sexual encounters by hiding in the library for much of the time. That had changed in the summer between his second and third year. He had bought a Eurail pass and spent eight weeks and too much money backpacking around the cities of Europe.

It was at the Berlin Opera House that he met Bernhardt. Dominic had been unsuccessfully trying to get a cheap ticket for a production of *La Bohème* when a voice behind him said, "It's a beautiful story and I want to help a beautiful man like you to see it." Dominic had turned to stare straight into the vivid blue eyes of a smartly dressed German man. He was probably only a few years older than the twenty-year-old Dominic.

His world changed that summer. It was a muddled, confused time. On the one hand, it brought bliss with the beautiful, tall, blond Bernhardt. On the other it brought terror at the prospect of coming out to his friends and family in England. It was a piece of drama that he could not face.

Dominic felt sublime that night as he watched Puccini's masterpiece at the Berlin State Opera House with Bernhardt next to him. They spent fifteen tempestuous nights together. Bernhardt was endlessly seductive and often explosive. He lived in a Bohemian apartment in the increasingly fashionable area of East Berlin. His parents were very wealthy, and

Bernhardt was not without money. With wealth came an arrogance and dominance in their fledgling relationship that Dominic found at first seductive but ultimately unbearable.

On the sixteenth night, while Bernhardt went to cruise the bars of Schöneberg, Dominic packed his rucksack and took the U-Bahn to the Hauptbahnhof. There he took an overnight train to Prague. Two friends from university had been planning a trip there, and Dominic vainly hoped he might bump into them for some familiar company and a sympathetic shoulder to cry on. He got a bed in the YMCA in Na Poříčí, just off the Old Town Square, where he stayed for four nights before a longing to return to the UK overwhelmed him and he set off on the journey back home.

The Berlin experience left him hopelessly confused. He was unhappy for a long time. In the years to follow, he was to have many regrets about that summer. The main one being that when he returned to England, he had not come out to his family. It was only after another six months that he confided in close friends so that at least in their company he could be comfortable and satisfied with who he was. When he thought hard about it, it was only since his relationship with Jonathan that he had started to reach the contentment he sought, seventeen years after that summer traveling Europe.

Dominic's phone began ringing and jolted him out of his reminiscence. It was Jonathan.

"Where the hell are you, lover?"

12

BY THREE thirty in the morning, Jonathan and Dominic were curled up on the settee in the front room of Jonathan's tiny cottage in Lewes. They had vainly tried to stoke life back into the dying embers of the log burner. The room was rapidly losing its warmth, but Dominic still had adrenaline coursing in his veins from the evening's revelations. Jonathan seemed happy to massage his partner's neck as Dominic went over the night's events.

"I don't think it means Simon is a blackmailer at all," mused Dominic, rolling a brandy glass in his left hand to warm it. "I'm not sure about this housemate, Jay. He's a volatile character, and there seems little love lost between him and the others. We only have his word that he found those photographs in Simon's room and concealed them from the police."

"Are you saying he planted them to frame Simon? If so, why didn't he just leave them in the room to be discovered?" asked Jonathan.

John's revelation of what he had found in the rucksack had been a bombshell to everyone. Inside was an A4 manila envelope of freeze-frame photographic images, apparently taken from several surveillance cameras in what looked like the room of a stately home. The photographs showed several men engaged in vigorous sexual activities. Inside the envelope was a scrap of paper on which was typed:

Meet you at the location as agreed. Be alone, we'll be watching.

"But what if the rucksack wasn't in Simon's room but in Jay's, and Jay simply claimed that it was in Simon's room? What if Jay is actually the blackmailer?" asked Dominic.

"If he is the blackmailer, then why show the rucksack to John? Surely he'd want to hang on to it to collect the spoils?" replied Jonathan, rubbing Dominic's neck absently. "No, I think this gives someone an ideal motive to want Simon dead and explains the two attempts on his life. Using ketamine as the murder weapon, the murderer hoped to make it look like Simon had simply overdosed. Our man Mr. Freedman with the syringe at the hospital proved that. It's clear that when Simon was first found in the house, someone—probably Freedman—had tried to kill him."

"All of this has got to be reported to the police now. I can't be party to withholding evidence any longer," said Dominic decisively. "When we go to the police station tomorrow morning, we're going to have to tell them we were chasing Freedman when he ran out in front of that car. And we must tell them about this blackmail evidence. It's going to be devastating news for Samantha. I must talk to her first." He sighed. "I have to go back home tomorrow as well. I can't be out of the office any longer; I'll lose what remaining clients I have."

Dominic leaned back against Jonathan's massaging fingers. He was dreading the thought of returning to

Oxfordshire and being apart from Jonathan. Choosing to live separately had seemed the sensible thing to do while they were unsure of their relationship. But tonight, lying in his lover's arms sipping a brandy, he felt content and certain that he wanted to move on from a weekend relationship. He was nervous about discussing the idea with Jonathan. He was still afraid he might be rejected. Perhaps the early hours of the morning were not the time to start talking about it. Instead he asked, "Where are the photos and list of names now?"

"John's keeping them close to him. His charming friend Steve seems to think that they could be some kind of bargaining tool. God knows how. He says the two of them are going to research the names and faces on the internet. However, I did happen to have my mobile with me, and as you know, I take a mean photograph...." As he spoke Jonathan tugged the little phone out of his pocket and brought up a series of images on the screen.

"Why didn't you tell me before?" cried Dominic, turning round to peer at the screen.

"Do you know just how late it is?" asked Jonathan wearily. "We have to get up again in a few short hours to go down to the police station to meet those two charming juvenile police officers. Can't we leave our own continuing investigations until the morning?"

But Dominic had taken the phone from Jonathan's outstretched hand and was flicking through the images. Despite being a good photographer, the task of sneaking clandestine shots of documents and photos in a nightclub appeared to be beyond even Jonathan's skills. He had made several attempts at photographing the list of names, but the combination of a tiny screen, poor focus, and a shaky hand made it impossible for Dominic to read any of them. He flicked to the photographs and enlarged one of them on the screen, sliding it around to look at the slightly fuzzy image.

"Goodness, they are having fun, aren't they?" he murmured as he tried to distinguish the blurry faces. There was one man who seemed to be less involved in the group activity than the rest. Dominic felt sure he had seen him before. He flicked through the images to try to get a clearer view, but the man always appeared on the edge of the frame with his face partially obscured, or he had his back to the camera.

"There's something about this one," he indicated to Jonathan. "I'm sure I've seen him somewhere before, but I can't get a clear enough view of his face."

"And I always thought you'd led such a sheltered life, my dear," Jonathan whispered into his ear. "If I'd known that you were into group sex, then I'd have introduced you to some acquaintances a long time ago."

Dominic laughed and nestled back into Jonathan. He held the mobile above his head so that they both could see it. With his thumb he pointed at the edge of the screen.

"To be honest it's difficult to work out whether this is group sex or a game of naked rugby in some stately home. You take a look at the chap on the far left of this photo. It's almost like he knows where the security cameras are and is keeping out of view, but here he's obviously got a bit distracted...."

"Probably by the cute young thing sucking his cock, I'd imagine," replied Jonathan drolly. "Lover, it really is too late to be looking at security-video porn. Let's wait until the morning when we can transfer it onto the large computer screen."

Jonathan gently took the phone from Dominic's hand and put it on the table behind him. "Bedtime, my little

Hercule Poirot. Unless you would like us to have our own security-video moment now." He reached down and began to unbutton the fly of Dominic's trousers. "Goodness, I think you do," he exclaimed with mock surprise. "I think you'd better let me see to that now. It wouldn't do for you to walk into Brighton police station tomorrow morning with your trousers in such a state, now would it?"

THE ALARM sounded at seven thirty the next morning. Dominic groaned, but Jonathan continued to sleep. Reaching his arm out from beneath the warm duvet into the cold air of the bedroom, Dominic fumbled for the alarm clock. He cursed Jonathan for not installing central heating in the two-hundred-year-old cottage. As he silenced the alarm, his mobile phone began to ring on the nightstand beside the bed. Dominic considered leaving it for a moment, but curiosity got the better of him, and he picked up the call.

"Is that Mr. Dominic Delingpole?" asked a man's voice at the other end of the line.

"Yes. Who's this?" replied Dominic warily.

"I'm Constable Locking from Thames Valley Police. I'm sorry to say that we received a report of a break-in at your apartment in Ash House last night. Miss Alexis Bunce from number three in your apartment block contacted us when she saw signs of a forced entry to your front door."

"Last night?" interrupted Dominic. "Why didn't you call me earlier?"

"Miss Bunce reported the break-in at 11:00 p.m. last night. We attended at 11:25 p.m. and, having ascertained that there was no one present in the property, we arranged for the door to be made secure," continued the officer. He was clearly affronted by Dominic's outburst. "We felt that it was best to wait until morning before contacting you so that you might get some sleep. I've been on the night shift here, sir," added Constable Locking for good measure.

"Thank you, Officer, that was thoughtful of you," replied Dominic wearily. "Have they stolen anything?"

"That is not something we are able to ascertain, sir, and why we will need your presence at the property. Miss Bunce informed us that you might be away as a result of the incident involving Mrs. Gregory in the upstairs apartment. If you would be so kind as to give us your estimated return date, then we can arrange for someone to meet you at your property to facilitate access, seeing as how the door has been sealed up to prevent further intrusions at this moment in time."

Dominic wished that the British police force could be taught to speak normal, everyday English. As he ended the call, Jonathan stirred next to him. "Who on earth is calling at this ungodly hour?" he mumbled.

"It's getting on for eight," replied Dominic, shivering his way out of bed. "We've got to be at the police station by nine. That was the police back home. The apartment's been burgled."

Jonathan sat up. "Oh my God, what is going on? Have they stolen anything?"

"The police don't know, so I've got to get back there as soon as I can. It never rains but it pours, does it? If the collection's gone, I don't think I'll stop crying for a week."

Dominic had amassed a considerable collection of art deco glassware over the years. There were only a few pieces of real value, but it was the beauty of the objects that he cherished more. Nagging at the back of his mind was the thought that the burglary might have something to do with the events surrounding Simon Gregory. For the moment he dismissed the thoughts from his mind as creeping paranoia. Anyway, he had more important things to worry about. There was the very real threat of being charged with withholding evidence. He was not relishing the visit to Brighton police station.

———

WHEN JONATHAN, Dominic, and Christophe met up at the police station, they were told that neither Sergeant Dixon nor Constable Crawford were available. Instead, they were shown into an interview room by a tall, distinguished-looking officer.

"My name is Detective Inspector Scott," he began, revealing a Highland accent to match his name. "This shouldn't take long. Just a few formalities. Now, you were present at the incident in Old Steine last night when the gentleman was hit by a black Range Rover car. What were the three of you doing in the area at that time?"

"Oh, you know, Inspector, just passing through," said Jonathan airily. "We were thinking of going for a sauna actually." Dominic groaned inwardly. He would have preferred Jonathan to be a little more discreet, but perhaps honesty was a better approach.

"An interesting coincidence. It seems that the victim had just visited the Sauna Bar. Did you know the man?"

Jonathan jumped in before Dominic had a chance to answer. "No, Detective Inspector. We saw that the man was running ahead of us, and then a few moments later we heard the crash." Dominic was briefly annoyed at Jonathan's intervention. Although not a lie, his remarks withheld significant amounts of the truth. Dominic had prepared himself to reveal all that they knew to this officer.

"I see," mused DI Scott. "Unfortunately we're having difficulty identifying the man. Strangely we found no form of identification on him, and as you probably know—" He paused, looking directly at Dominic. "—the Sauna Bar is entirely anonymous. We're running checks on his fingerprints and dental records at the moment."

Dominic's heart missed several beats, and he looked across at Christophe. He was sure he had seen Christophe put the wallet back into Peter Freedman's pocket shortly before the ambulance turned up. Why had the police not found it on the dead man? He glanced at Jonathan, whose face betrayed no hint of emotion. Dominic's intentions to tell everything to the police now completely deserted him. The new information from DI Scott confused him, and he was relieved that Jonathan had intervened a moment earlier. His lawyer instincts encouraged him to maintain his silence, painfully aware that the police officer was still staring at him.

Detective Inspector Scott paused a moment longer before continuing, "It's very unusual to find no identification. Usually there's a driving licence or a credit card. He didn't even have a wallet. But I suppose men that visit those sorts of places often have things to hide."

DI Scott continued to look squarely at Dominic with his piercing blue eyes. "You gave our officers your statements last night. Is there anything you might be able to add this morning?"

Dominic decided that, as the unappointed lawyer for the three, he should answer before Jonathan had a chance to say anything more.

"I'm afraid there's really nothing to add. We did our best

to help, but there was really not much we could do before the ambulance arrived." He looked at D I Scott across the table without blinking. Under different circumstances he would have found the inspector's blue eyes and square jaw particularly seductive. "Perhaps he'd lost his wallet or it had been stolen, Detective Inspector?"

DI Scott paused again and then said, "Well, we've spoken to the driver of the vehicle that hit the deceased. You met Mr. Faldon, I believe. He says that the man simply ran out into the road in front of him, and that he had no time to stop. It seems this was simply a tragic accident."

Dominic glanced at Jonathan, who by now was industriously cleaning some gardening dirt from under his fingernails. He looked back at DI Scott, who held his gaze steadily. Finally the Detective Inspector pushed back his chair and stood up.

"Thank you, gentlemen. That will be all for the moment. We have your contact details. If we have any further questions, we'll be in touch."

He turned to leave the room and then looked around at Dominic to ask, "By the way, who made the emergency call last night? Was it you?"

"No," replied Dominic. "It was the driver."

"Hmm, interesting," replied DI Scott. "Well, that will be all." He held the door open for the three men and escorted them back to the main entrance of the police station.

STANDING OUTSIDE the police station, the cold December wind whipping their faces, Dominic turned to Christophe. "You did put that wallet back in his pocket, didn't you? I saw you do it."

Christophe opened his mouth to reply but was interrupted by Jonathan, who was wrapping his Abercrombie & Fitch jacket tightly around his body to keep out the cold. "My dear, it's very clear. There's some kind of conspiracy going on here, and I don't think that even the lovely old police know what's going on. Old Scottie dog back there was as puzzled as you or I. The wallet on that man showed he was called Peter Freedman and that he had some connection with the House of Commons. Darling Christophe certainly put the wallet back into Freedman's pocket just as the ambulance arrived. Somewhere between the ambulance people picking up the body and the police getting involved, that wallet went missing. It wouldn't have dropped out, so someone must have taken it. Someone who didn't want Freedman's identity known. This is just too exciting. Let's go and get a drink to warm up and work out what we know."

Dominic shook his head. "I've got to get back to Oxfordshire. Don't forget that someone's broken into the apartment. I need to find out what's happened." He turned to face Jonathan directly, holding his partner's hands in his, and chose his next words carefully. "I'm sorry, Jonathan, I don't feel your same thrill for this. You're right to say that we're involved in some kind of conspiracy, but I'm afraid that it could hurt us all if we're not careful. There's a boy unconscious in hospital, a man dead, and my apartment's been burgled. You've got some bizarre pornographic images on your phone, which may or may not be a case of blackmail that's linked into all of this, and we now know a bunch of students who could be involved in some strange drug trials."

Without hesitation Jonathan leaned forward and kissed him gently on the lips. He pulled Dominic against him in an affectionate, warming embrace. As they hugged, Jonathan spoke directly into his ear.

"Lover, you're right. I know. I'm being flippant and trivial. There's one person who's stuck right in the middle of this through no choice of her own. Darling Samantha is all alone at that hospital, not knowing whether her son will ever regain consciousness. For her sake, we must get to the bottom of this. I might act silly and excited, but my heart's in the right place."

Dominic allowed himself to relax into Jonathan's body for a few moments before straightening up, shivering slightly in the winter wind.

"Oh, Jonathan, your heart is always in the right place. And you're right about Samantha. She brought us here to start with, and we can't let her down now. I need something warm before heading back to the apartment." Jonathan's tongue caressed his ear. "And no, I don't mean that. Let's treat ourselves to coffee and cake at the Grand Hotel on the seafront before I go. We can make a plan together. You know that always makes me happy."

THE REVOLVING door of the Grand spun the three men into a warm foyer and the sudden hush of hotel aristocracy. A thick pile carpet led away towards a high-ceilinged dining room. Its brightly lit tables were filled with the subdued hubbub of mid-morning ladies who lunched, mingling with smart-suited business executives armed with laptops and mobile phones.

A liveried waiter escorted them to a white linen covered table in the corner. Jonathan drew some disapproving stares as he walked through the elegant room. His gardening trousers, army boots, and motorbike jacket contrasted with the sober clothing of the Grand's clientele. Jonathan cheerfully smiled and waved at anyone who glanced in his direction. They, in turn, hastily looked away. As the three approached their table, Jonathan suddenly peeled off to greet one of the diners noisily.

"Mrs. de Valles! How absolutely wonderful to see you! How is the new pond doing this winter? Have you avoided it icing up in this dreadful weather?"

A red-haired woman in her sixties turned, and her eyes lit up when she saw Jonathan.

"Dear boy, my wonderful gardening angel!" Chatter on the tables around Mrs. de Valles hushed as several heads turned to see the incongruous meeting between the doyenne of South Downs society and what appeared to be a dispatch rider without his helmet. Mrs. de Valles turned to her dining companion.

"Cynthia, this adorable man is responsible single-handedly for the transformation of the grounds of the hall into the delightful home for my garden parties. Jonathan McFadden, this is Cynthia Palmer-Edwards. You two really must talk sometime."

"Cynthia Palmer-Edwards of *Gossip!* magazine? What scurrilous stories are you digging up with poor innocent Constanza here?" Jonathan struck a dramatic pose. "I should throw myself between you to defend her reputation before you wreak havoc in her genteel, reclusive life."

A few feet away, Dominic stood patiently with Christophe, watching his partner flirt effortlessly. The women laughed at Jonathan's harmless mischief, each touching him on the arm as he crouched down at the table between them. Dominic wished that he had the charm and chutzpah that allowed Jonathan to develop new business contacts so easily.

"Well, my dear man, perhaps I'll write about you and

your cavalier gardening exploits next month. Didn't D. H. Lawrence write about someone like you in *Lady Chatterley's Lover*?" Cynthia Palmer-Edwards clasped Jonathan's bicep in her hand. "That's not a bad idea of mine. Constanza, you must give me this delightful man's contact details. The gardener's view of Sussex society. It would work well in the spring edition. And who are these other two charming gentlemen, Mr....?"

"Jonathan McFadden at your service, ma'am." Jonathan gently prized the firm grip of her fingers from his upper arm and brought her hand up to his lips to kiss it.

"Allow me to introduce you to Dominic Delingpole, lawyer extraordinary and my darling partner of several years. And this is Christophe LeBatier, security consultant and man of muscle."

A flicker of sexual disappointment betrayed itself in the eyes of Cynthia Palmer-Edwards for just a moment before she adopted a serene expression and smiled sweetly at Dominic and Christophe. "I'm enchanted to meet you all. Particularly you, Mr. McFadden. Here's my card. We must meet again very soon."

The three men took seats at their own table, and Dominic leaned over to Jonathan.

"It constantly amazes me to watch you in action. You charm the birds from the trees. If she does that piece on you in *Gossip!* Magazine, you'll have work coming out of your ears. Although now she's met me, I think she's cooled a bit."

"Oh, I don't think so. Women like that love the company of gay men. All the fun of flirtation with none of the unpleasant follow-through. She was very quick to give me her card." Jonathan picked up the menu. "Now, what are we all having? My treat, seeing as I may become outrageously rich very soon." Jonathan grinned broadly. "Bacon sandwich and a cup of tea for me, I think. What about you, Christophe?"

The Frenchman snorted loudly. "Bread, butter, and greasy English bacon. That is not the way to eat healthily, so that is certainly not for me." As he was saying this, Jonathan leaned over and massaged Christophe's pectoral muscle. "Hmm, cantaloupe and a glass of hot water for you, then, my man of muscle." Jonathan glanced over at Dominic's disapproving look. "Earl Grey and a large slice of lemon for you, lover?"

Before Dominic could answer, his mobile rang. After a short conversation, he carefully put the phone on the table before turning to Jonathan. "That was Samantha. Simon's condition has got worse. It looks like he might not survive."

13

"WHY ARE those disgusting pictures still here?"

Gemma walked across to the sink, a battered electric kettle in her hand. As she passed John seated at the kitchen table, she briefly peered over his shoulder. He was sifting through an array of lurid photographs. There were more than twenty, A4 size images. When he glanced up, Gemma quickly turned back to the overflowing sink. She filled the kettle and sought out the least dirty coffee mugs.

"What if the police come back now?" she continued. "You've got to get rid of them, John, otherwise you'll be in the shit."

"I'm not getting rid of them. They're the reason Si's in hospital, I'm sure of it. What I don't get is why they were under Si's bed."

"If they were under Si's bed," interrupted Gemma.

John turned to stare at her.

"Well, I mean," continued Gemma, "how do we know they were there? Did you know they were there?"

"I didn't make a habit of looking under Si's bed...," began John.

"No, you were doing more interesting things with Si in it." Jay entered the kitchen, crossed to the fridge, and took out a bottle of protein shake. Gemma watched him nervously as he took a long draft from the bottle, replaced it, and closed the fridge door. His eyes met hers, and they stared at each other for a moment.

"So what are you saying, Gemma? That I'm a liar?"

The kettle boiled and poured steam into the atmosphere as its ancient switch refused to turn off.

"Oh shit, look at this." John had been holding a magnifying glass over one of the photographs. He looked up, and his face was ashen. "It's Si, I'm sure of it."

Jay walked over to the table and took the photograph and magnifying glass from John's hand.

"Look at the far left," John directed. "There's a mirror over the fireplace. You can see Si's face reflected in it."

Gemma's curiosity got the better of her revulsion. She finally succeeded in switching off the erupting kettle and turned to the table. The photograph in Jay's hand was taken from the high vantage point of a security camera. It showed one section of a large oak-panelled room. There were two long maroon settees in the shot, positioned on either side of a Victorian high-mantel fireplace. Two naked men were coupled on the settee to the left of the fireplace. One faced the camera, astride the other man, who lay flat on the settee. In the foreground she could see the heads of three other men, their faces hidden from the camera.

Jay held the magnifying glass over the image of the mirror above the fireplace.

"My God, Jay. Do you like your pornography close up?" Gemma asked.

Jay ignored her question, "I don't think I can look at this anymore." But his actions contradicted his words. He seemed fascinated by the image in front of him. Finally, with impatience, Gemma took the magnifying glass from his hand.

"Oh right, sister. Not so disgusted now, are we? It's fucking weird, that."

Gemma ignored him and looked closely at the mirror in the photograph. She could see the reflected shapes of at least half a dozen naked men. All except one of them was engaged in feverish sexual activity. That younger man was standing stock-still. He faced the mirror in apparent detachment from what was going on around him. He looked very like Simon Gregory.

Gemma handed the magnifying glass back to Jay. "I suppose it could be him. It's not very clear, though."

Jay examined the photograph again. "Voyeur at an orgy in an English stately home? Or participant? This is a whole other side to Simon that I bet you didn't know about, John. Yeah, I reckon it could be him. It's not very clear, but after the sick stuff that's been happening in the last few days, I'd believe anything—"

There were tears forming in John's eyes. "Fuck off, Jay." He turned to Gemma. "There's a mark on Si's right shoulder. It's a birthmark. He's kind of proud of it for some weird reason. You can see the same mark on the guy in the photograph."

Gemma snatched the magnifying glass back from Jay and re-examined the photograph closely.

"It might not be a birthmark on the guy's shoulder. It could just be something on the image. It does look a lot like Si, I suppose, but—"

"I know it's him. Of course it's him. But what the fuck is he doing there?"

John stood up suddenly, his chair clattering over on the

grubby tile floor. He stalked out of the kitchen, and a moment later they heard his feet thudding up the stairs.

Jay picked up the manila envelope that had held the photographs. He pulled out the scrappy piece of paper inside and reread the words typed on it:

Meet you at the location as agreed. Be alone, we'll be watching.

He threw the paper back down on the table. "Si's in some serious shit. Up to his neck. But what the hell's he doing? Think about it. He's at this orgy in this posh place. God knows why. He sees famous people there, perhaps. And he sees there are security cameras. God knows why the other bozos getting their rocks off didn't spot them. Maybe they were too busy having a fucking good time. Anyhow. Simon manages to get hold of the pictures from the camera, 'cause he knows he could be in them. Perhaps he plans to destroy them so there's no evidence of him there. Then he has an idea: he could blackmail the famous people caught on the security cameras...."

"Oh, come off it, Jay." Gemma turned back to the sink and switched the kettle on again. "Surely it's the other way round. How's Simon going to get to the security cameras? They'd be under the control of someone who's in that place, wherever it is. Maybe they own it or something. It's much more likely it's someone there who's trying to blackmail Si."

"That doesn't make any sense." Jay picked up the photograph again. He seemed to be becoming fascinated with the orgy. "Si's not worth blackmailing. He's not got any money, as far as I know. His mum's a widow, isn't she? When he got hold of this stuff, I bet the temptation was just too great. I reckon John's golden boy is more than a little tarnished...."

Gemma slammed the coffee jar down on the worktop.

"Make your own bloody coffee, Jay. That's when you've finished getting your own rocks off on those photos." She left the kitchen and ran up the stairs.

John was sitting on the bed in Simon's room, his back to the door, when Gemma found him. She stood in the doorway, breathing deeply. She wished they had never picked Jay as one of their housemates.

"You okay, John?"

"I don't know what to think anymore," John answered. "Two days ago I loved Si more than anyone I've ever known. I haven't stopped loving him, but...."

Gemma crossed the room and sat on the bed next to John. She put her arm around him, and he rested his head on her shoulder. They sat in silence for a few moments, John's body shaking gently with suppressed tears.

Finally Gemma spoke. "I believe in him still. He's not a blackmailer. He's an innocent. He's naïve, an idealist. God, you've said that to me before, John. You know, I think we're forgetting something about Simon." She turned to look at John. "What does Simon want to be more than anything in the world?"

John lifted his head from her shoulder. "A journalist! Fuck, you're right."

He jumped up and crossed to a dark, ugly-looking wardrobe on the far side of the room. He reached up and pulled down a khaki computer holdall, then sat down next to Gemma again, unzipped the holdall, and pulled out a battered laptop.

"I'm going to find out who these people are and where they are. The pictures are the key to finding out who's trying to kill him."

"So what are you going to do, John? Hack into his laptop?" The voice came from the doorway. They both turned to see Jay standing there, with three mugs of coffee in his hands and the envelope of photographs under his arm.

"I don't need to. I know his password." John's fingers clattered across the keyboard. "Somewhere in here has to be a file, an e-mail, something that will help us find out where that place is." He turned to Jay. "Are you going to help me, or are you going to assume the worst of Si?"

Jay set the coffee mugs down on the desk by the window. "I wanna know the answers, mate. If Simon was playing at journalists"— Jay threw the envelope on the bed beside John—"then we could have the scoop of the century here."

John stopped typing for a moment. He reached into his pocket and pulled out a battered mobile phone. He looked up triumphantly at Jay and Gemma. "And if we don't find enough on the laptop, we can get to work on Si's phone. We'll find out who the bastards are behind all this."

14

DOMINIC'S DRIVE back to Oxfordshire was slow. An accident brought the traffic to a standstill, and his silver Audi crawled along the M25 for several miles. No sooner had he cleared the accident and resumed a decent speed, than he was brought back to a crawl at the usual bottleneck around Heathrow airport. It added nearly an hour to the journey from Brighton to his Oxfordshire home.

He used the extra time to make a series of calls and deal with the most pressing matters at work. Gillian offered to meet him at the apartment, an offer he gratefully accepted —partly because it meant he could deal with a few more items of work, but mainly because he wanted another professional person who he could trust to help him deal with the officious police officer, Locking, who would be waiting for him. Gillian had a key to the apartment and could let herself in. Dominic was confident she would take charge of the situation.

"I'll tell the young police officer to meet me there at eleven, and I'll settle him down with coffee and a biscuit before you get here," she had said. "Hopefully by the time you arrive, all you'll need to do is a quick check around to see what's missing, if anything. Then let him know and we can send him on his way."

Gillian had worked for Dominic for over ten years. He never failed to admire her ability to organize his life. She left him space to be cerebral. Several years ago he had realized that he could confidently let her handle many aspects of his routine legal work. That allowed him to deal with the more challenging and interesting aspects of his job.

As Dominic pulled the convertible into the driveway of his apartment house off the High Street, he thought about how he had left Samantha just after she received the news of her son's worsening condition. He felt guilty about his decision, but reassured himself that Jonathan had promised to meet her at the hospital later in the day. By then Christophe would be back on duty in the hospital's basement security office.

He switched off the engine, heaved a sigh of relief, and sat for a moment in the dark leather cocoon of his car. A police car was already in the parking bay alongside him. Reaching behind his seat for the Louis Vuitton overnight bag Jonathan had bought him for their first anniversary, he took a deep breath and climbed out of the car.

THE FIRST thing Dominic saw as he walked into the entrance hall of Ash House that morning was the damage to his front door. The heavy oak frame had been splintered around the main lock and top bolt. Someone had rather clumsily added a heavy-duty hasp and eye to the door to make it temporarily secure. Dominic's heart sank when he saw the additional damage this security measure had caused to the doorframe.

Standing in the hallway was one of the two athletically built officers who had delivered the bad news about Simon to Samantha Gregory just two days ago. At least this was welcome eye candy after the gruelling journey home.

The officer was wearing a long-sleeved blue shirt under his stab vest. It pulled tightly around his biceps, and Dominic could see the hint of a tattoo on the top part of his right arm.

"Good morning, Mr. Delingpole," the officer said. "I'm Constable Jansen. I'm sorry that we have to meet again so soon."

Dominic was hesitant to agree with that sentiment. In his view the young man was extremely fit and had a strong grip as they shook hands.

At that moment Gillian emerged from his apartment into the hallway.

"Good morning, Dominic. I can see that you've met Constable Jansen." She gave Dominic a disapproving look. "Will you be staying out here with him for the morning or will you come through for some coffee? I took the liberty of brewing a cafetière for us. I thought that you might be in need of a cup. Here's your mail. Two bills, by the look of them, and this package. By the way, Detective Fairburn is in the living room waiting for you."

Gillian handed the two envelopes and a brown paper parcel to Dominic and swept back into the apartment.

Dominic turned to Constable Jansen, whose steely blue eyes had begun to fascinate him. "Are you coming in as well, Officer?"

"No, sir. I have to talk to the other residents here, those that are in. We're not sure how the intruder managed to enter the building to start with. There's no sign of a forced entry to the front door, or anywhere else for that matter. It's only your apartment that's had the door broken down, I'm afraid."

At that moment the front door of Ash House burst open and the burly, be-suited frame of Randolph James strode into the hallway.

"Good God, what's happened? A break-in? Is it just you or have they done the other apartments as well?"

Constable Jansen stepped forward. "Do you live here, sir?"

"Yes, Officer. Number four, upstairs. I'm Randolph James, MP. My constituency's up in Yorkshire, but I keep this handy pied-a-terre. Prefer to be just outside London, even if it's still a commute to Parliament. So, have I been done over too?"

"No sir, only Mr. Delingpole's apartment has been targeted." He turned to Dominic. "Would either of you happen to know how many people have keys for the main front door of the house? At the moment we can only conclude that the intruder managed to obtain a key from somewhere."

"My dear chap, there must be hundreds of people who have keys to the front door," said Randolph James impatiently. "Apart from the residents, their families, and sundry others, there are cleaners, the occasional tradesmen, and goodness knows who else. It's open house, virtually. That's why we have decent locks and security on our own front doors." He glanced at Dominic briefly. "Sorry, old chap, seems like yours let you down. Know what they got?"

Before Dominic could answer, a woman wearing what he considered to be a very unflattering trouser suit stepped out of his apartment. Constable Jansen visibly straightened his back and his very broad shoulders at the arrival of Detective Fairburn.

"Ma'am. This is the owner, Mr. Delingpole. And this is—"

"Randolph James," interrupted the MP. "I have a little apartment upstairs. Any chance we can keep this low-key? Don't want my constituents up in Yorkshire thinking their own MP is incapable of keeping decent security. The press there would have a field day, I'm certain. Particularly as I've been banging on about Britain's security for the last year and a half."

Detective Fairburn ignored the MP's extended hand of greeting and turned instead to Dominic.

"Mr. Delingpole. I'm Detective Wendy Fairburn. I'm sorry to have to meet you under these circumstances. Would you mind coming into your apartment to answer a few questions? We'd very much like to find out if you believe anything is missing, to help us establish some kind of motive."

She turned to Randolph James. "I'd be grateful if you'd remain available for the next hour, Mr. James. I'll be coming to ask you a few questions after I've finished with Mr. Delingpole." And before the MP could reply, she turned to go back into Dominic's apartment.

"Damn it, I've got my driver waiting outside...."

Detective Fairburn turned in the doorway. "Well, if that's the case, then we'll come and look for you at the Houses of Parliament. But then that would make it harder for you to 'keep it low-key,' wouldn't it? The choice is yours."

Then Detective Fairburn turned to Dominic. "Mr. Delingpole, shall we?" She ushered Dominic into his own apartment.

Although he had been steeling himself for the mess he

might encounter, Dominic was still shocked by what he saw. It seemed that nothing had been left untouched. Papers from his study were scattered throughout the hallway. A large art deco mirror that hung over the radiator was smashed. Dominic looked in through the doorway of his small study off the hall. Almost every book had been swept off the shelves. Drawers hung out of the filing cabinet, their contents spilling onto the floor. For a moment he steadied himself against the doorframe before pulling himself upright.

"Detective, it will take me some time to go through this. Frankly, it will be difficult to work out what might be missing. I've accumulated rather a lot over the past few years."

"I understand, Mr. Delingpole. Tell me, did you have any computer equipment here?"

Dominic smiled. "I'm a rather old-fashioned person in that regard, Detective. I try to leave the technology at the office with Gillian. I have succumbed to one of those tablet things on which I now have to read documents, but that's never left here. I suppose I keep rather more paper than perhaps I should." He surveyed the mess in front of them. "Perhaps now is the time for a little spring cleaning."

Sighing, Dominic bent down to a piece of stiff parchment poking out from a smashed picture frame. "My graduation certificate. Rather foolish sentimentality to have framed it, I suppose." He stood up. "I think I need that coffee now."

They went into the sitting room. Watery December sunlight filtered in through the French windows that opened onto the gardens of Ash House. Gillian poured him a coffee. Surprisingly, the living room was largely untouched. Dominic's collection of CDs was scattered across the parquet floor. Pictures had been taken from the walls, and bizarrely, the coal bucket was upended over the hearthrug. With relief Dominic saw that his collection of art deco cocktail glasses remained untouched in the cabinet by the fireplace. The room was sparingly furnished. There were two cream leather settees and a high-backed wing armchair to the side of the French windows. Dominic settled into the armchair, gratefully accepting a cup of black coffee from Gillian.

"We don't believe this was a robbery, Mr. Delingpole," Detective Fairburn said. "The common items that thieves target are all still here. Do you have a safe in the apartment?"

Dominic shook his head. "The only things of real value are that collection of glassware and this armchair. It's a Rennie Mackintosh," he added, by way of explanation.

Detective Fairburn perched on the corner of one of the settees, declining a cup of coffee from Gillian. "You're a lawyer, I understand. Do you have any clients with a grudge?"

"Well, they're usually unhappy about something. It's the rich pattern of my work with the great British public. But this...." Dominic gestured at the room. "This is a little extreme."

He took a sip of his coffee. It was already clear in his mind that the recent events in Brighton were related to the ransacking of his apartment. But after the bizarre interview with Detective Inspector Scott that morning, Dominic had no intention of confiding his suspicions to the young woman who sat across from him. Instead he asked, "I presume that you checked for fingerprints, footprints, the usual evidence like that?"

"Yes, we've already done that. It's normal procedure when criminal damage is involved. However, it's more than likely that the intruder, or intruders, wore gloves." Detective Fairburn stood up. "We'll leave you to check for anything that's missing. Do let us know, won't you?"

She walked towards the door before turning back to Dominic. "By the way, I received a call from Sussex Police shortly before you arrived. They told me that you're representing Mrs. Samantha Gregory. Is that so?"

Dominic nodded but chose to say nothing, waiting to see what might come next.

"Has it not crossed your mind that the same people who attempted to murder her son might also be connected to this?" She gestured around her. "I hope that you might give me more complete answers when we next meet. It's good news on Simon Gregory. He recovered consciousness half an hour ago. Good-bye, Mr. Delingpole."

15

SAMANTHA GREGORY sat on one of the hard plastic chairs in the corridor outside Simon's room. She had been there for nearly an hour. Screens were pulled around his bed, and Samantha felt like a spectator at some bizarre medical pantomime. Three or four nursing staff hurried back and forth, smiling reassuringly at her each time. She had watched a succession of doctors arrive and depart. In addition a policeman stood outside the door to Simon's room, checking the identities of anyone who entered.

It was just after lunchtime and she had been sitting by Simon's bed reading when her son stirred. She laid the book down, removed her reading glasses, and gazed at his pallid face on the pillow. Simon's eyelids were flickering, and his head was rolling gently from side to side.

Samantha reached across with her right hand and stroked his forehead, as she had done when he was a child. At the same time, she reached for the emergency pull cord with her left hand. An alarm began to sound, and within minutes the door opened and the ICU's duty sister walked in.

By this time it was clear that Simon was regaining consciousness. Samantha had been gently ushered out of the room as an increasing number of medical staff arrived. She wanted to call Dominic, but the battery on her mobile phone was dead. She longed for a cup of coffee but did not want to leave the ward.

Instead she sat staring through the window at the drama playing out before her. She rehearsed in her head the conversations she would have with Simon. She had so many questions, but she knew they would have to wait. Perhaps they might never be answered. She seemed to know so distressingly little about his life.

After her husband died in the climbing accident ten years before, Samantha had been forced to sell the large, comfortable detached house the family had enjoyed in the Cotswolds. Their modest two-bedroom apartment in Ash House was cramped by comparison. Samantha was concerned that she might become unfairly over dependent on their only son, who was now the man of the house. Perhaps it was the way she had behaved with him that led to the row they'd had on his seventeenth birthday. It was a trivial argument about the party she had planned. Simon had stormed out, and for the next year he had lived with the family of one of his school friends a few miles away.

Samantha had been devastated by Simon's rejection, endlessly questioning where she had gone wrong. The summer after his A-levels, Samantha had hardly seen him. He had gone to stay with friends in London, apparently sleeping on their couch and finding occasional bar work. He had sent her text messages from time to time. He only returned to Oxfordshire to get his A-level results from the school. They had gone for a celebratory drink, and she had tried to find out more about the friends he was living with.

At the start of their conversation, Simon had opened up and talked about his life in London. His friends had an apartment on the East side, close to Hackney. It was now a fast up-and-coming area since an urban regeneration scheme had transformed the area. His friends were two young men who worked for a television production company. They lived the dream that Simon aspired to.

When she asked more about his London housemates, Simon had become evasive, then hostile to her questioning. It was the first time that Samantha had guessed her son was gay. But during the entire conversation, she had avoided asking him directly.

Their celebration ended on a sour note. Simon walked out after accusing her of trying to interfere with his life. Samantha was left clutching her half-empty glass of champagne.

Perhaps she should have asked him more direct questions about his sexuality. Perhaps he had wanted her to do so. It was too late now. Too late to change history. Instead, if Simon pulled through, she hoped that they could build a better, more open relationship together.

"Mrs. Gregory, is everything all right? What's happening?" Samantha looked up to see Simon's housemate John and a young woman standing in the corridor.

The girl crouched down at Samantha's side. "Hi, I'm Gemma, one of Si's other housemates. I thought I'd come along with John this time. What's going on in there? Is Si going to be okay?"

Samantha began to recount the news to the two students. A nurse emerged from Simon's room.

"Mrs. Gregory? Would you like to come in now? We've had to sedate Simon, I'm afraid, because he was becoming very distressed with the tube in his throat. But he's doing a lot better. You can sit with him for a while. We'll review his situation again in an hour. If he continues to make progress, we can consider reducing the sedation."

Samantha put her hand on Gemma's shoulder. "You're very kind to come here, Gemma. I hoped that Simon had good friends at university. Now I know." As she stood up, she took John's hand. "I'm sorry. You've been texting me, and I must confess that I've not been answering. Give me some time with Simon. I promise that we can talk later, and you can tell me this important news you say you have."

Samantha let go of his hand and followed the nurse into Simon's room.

JOHN WALKED up to the window that separated them from Simon as Samantha entered the room. He placed the palm of his hand on the glass. His shoulders sagged as he looked at the almost lifeless form of his friend and lover lying in the bed beyond.

Gemma gently laid a hand on his shoulder. "Come on. Let's do something practical. You carry on working on deciphering those files you found on Si's laptop, and I'll go and get some coffee for all of us. I'm sure Si's mum could do with it."

John pulled away from the window and sat down heavily on one of the hard plastic seats. He heaved Simon's aging laptop out of his shoulder bag and opened up the screen. Ten minutes later, when Gemma returned with three plastic cups of hot brown liquid, he raised his face to her with a look of triumph.

"John, don't tell me you've cracked it! What have you found?" John beckoned Gemma to look at the screen. He was careful to keep it turned away from the police officer stationed by the door of Simon's room. John showed Gemma the list of addresses he had found.

"I knew this laptop would be treasure trove," he said with excitement. "I never really saw Si using it. He always seemed to be on the computers in the library. Just before we set off, I'd found some unusual hidden folders on the D drive. I never took Si to be a techie type. There's a lot I don't know about him, it seems. He's got address lists that would make your toes curl." There was a hint of admiration in his voice as he added, "He's going to be a great journalist, Gemma. Take a look at this."

Gemma set the cups of coffee down on the corridor floor and sat next to him. She leaned in to take a closer look at the screen. "It looks like a list of students—some of them have got halls of residence as their addresses. What's the big deal?"

John kept his voice low, conscious of the two policemen standing close by. "Yeah, they're students in the Barton Kane drug trials. You knew Si was into that. I'm one of their guinea pigs. He recruited me last year when I joined the house. Didn't he ever approach you?"

Gemma shook her head.

"Strange. Maybe you don't fit the profile or something. I knew that he must have something like this list hidden somewhere. But it's what I found with it that's the interesting bit."

John brought up a different address list on the screen. This time several of the names had companies listed alongside them.

"I want to know why Si has got the names and addresses of a bunch of company executives and what look like Members of Parliament on a list hidden in his laptop.

They're tied up with Barton Kane in some way, I'm sure of it. Si's put some cryptic notes alongside each of them. God, we really need to talk to him." John looked up at Simon's bed through the glass in front of them. "Do you think they'll let us in there?"

"It's going to be a while," Gemma said, "and I don't think Si's just going to open up to us about this, do you? He's kept it from us so far."

"But don't you see, this is all tied up with the attempts on his life!" John pointed at the screen as he continued in a whisper. "Look, this is some executive at Barton Kane. This guy is a junior minister in the Department of Health, and this is some other Member of Parliament. Si's got addresses, e-mail addresses, and even mobile phone numbers for them. If he's got those kinds of details, he's got to have been doing some serious snooping. I reckon Si's in deep shit here. We've got to help him. Otherwise they'll be coming for him again."

Gemma looked up at John. "Then we should go to the police. We could end up in as much danger as Si."

John shook his head. "At best we'd look like some anti-establishment, paranoid students. At worst, the police could be part of it as well. Our house has already been done over. What if the police are actually in on this?"

He stood up. "I'm going to talk to that lawyer friend of Mrs. Gregory's. I think we can trust him. But I haven't been able to get his contact details."

At that moment the door opposite swung open, and Samantha Gregory stepped out, her eyes red and puffy.

Gemma stood up. "Mrs. Gregory, is he going to be...?"

"It's too early to say, but...." She smiled. "I think things are better than they were a few hours ago. I'm going to sit down for a moment. I haven't slept for over a day. It's kind of you both to come. Simon is very lucky to have such good friends."

Samantha settled on the plastic seat vacated by Gemma a moment ago. Gemma handed her one of the cups of coffee she had brought back from the machine. "I'm afraid it might be a bit lukewarm now, Mrs. Gregory. I didn't want to barge in with it while you were in there."

As Samantha raised the cup to her lips, John stood up.

"We'll go now if that's all right, Mrs. Gregory. We can talk another time. It's not important now. Can we get you anything else before we go?"

"Could you call Dominic, er, Mr. Delingpole? The battery on my phone has died, and I haven't been able to recharge it. I'm going back to the hotel soon for some sleep, but I'd like to talk to him before I do and let him know the news."

"Yes, of course," said John, quickly taking out his mobile. Getting Dominic's phone number was too good an opportunity to miss. "Shall I dial it for you?"

Samantha handed him Dominic's business card. "Here. He's gone back home to Oxfordshire for a day or two. Something about a burglary at his apartment."

16

NOT LONG after Dominic finished the call with Samantha, his mobile phone rang again. The call was from the same number. "That didn't take long," he said brightly. "Are you missing me already?"

But it was a male voice that replied. "Actually, Mr. Delingpole, it's me. John. We, that is, Gemma and me, need to see you really urgently. Can you come back to Brighton any sooner?"

Dominic hesitated. He had still been recovering from the worrying encounter with Detective Fairburn when Samantha had reached him. She had confirmed the detective's information about Simon recovering consciousness. Dominic had promised her that he would return to Brighton as soon as he could. But first he had to finish checking through his possessions in the apartment. Then he had a number of clients to call back. Gillian could not fend them off forever.

"I can't come any sooner, John," he said. "I'm afraid there's an awful lot for me to do here."

"Well, can we come to see you? We've got something of Si's that you really ought to see."

"Can you tell me what it is?"

There was a pause. "I'd rather not on a mobile phone. You don't know who might be listening. Look, are you in London? We can get into Victoria station and meet you somewhere."

Detective Fairburn's passing remark about a link between the burglary and Simon Gregory's attackers had already unsettled Dominic. John's paranoia about the mobile phone added to his growing sense of unease. But it also sparked his curiosity.

Dominic had a meeting in London the next morning with the client who wanted to discuss his long-running patent dispute. The meeting was at offices in Holborn in Central London with a good friend of Dominic's. Miles Torrington QC was a lawyer. A barrister, to be precise, in the quaint way English law separated lawyers into barristers and solicitors. Miles and Dominic were at Oxford University at the same time. After graduating, Dominic plodded along as a provincial solicitor, dealing with clients with problems ranging from contract disputes to house purchases. Meanwhile, Miles chose to be a barrister, working in the courts day after day. He was a high flyer, and became one of the youngest QCs, or Queen's Counsels, in England. He specialized in forensic computer matters, or computer fraud, and his expertise was renowned in legal circles. He was just the person to talk to about the events in Brighton.

"I'm going to be with a barrister in London tomorrow," Dominic said to John. "You should meet him. He's got chambers in Lincoln's Inn. Join us there after lunch. I'll text you the address."

MILES AND Dominic spent over two hours in fraught discussion before they finally got rid of the demanding client. They agreed that the client's claim for breach of patent by a rival software company was a good one. But while Miles and Dominic recommended accepting a very generous offer of settlement, the client wanted to reject it and take the argument to court in the hope of winning more money.

"You know, Dominic," said Miles as he heaved at the drawer of a dilapidated filing cabinet. "It's no skin off my nose if the wretched client wants to waste his money on courts and judges and all." He pulled out a bottle of Glenfiddich and two glasses. "But why can't he see that he risks ending up with nothing? Why are clients always so convinced that they deserve their day in court?"

Dominic gratefully received the generous tumbler of Scotch and clinked glasses with Miles before replying. "I suppose for the same reason that people are desperate to be on television. It all looks so glamorous. The fact that most of them end up looking foolish seems to completely pass them by." He settled into the comfort of a large, slightly shabby Chesterfield sofa alongside Miles.

"My dear Dominic, you're so right. But thank God for the vanity of men. Otherwise my children's school fees would go unpaid. Now what's this about your adventures in the flesh-pots of Brighton? I always saw you as a stay-at-home queen. Don't tell me you've started clubbing! At your age?"

Dominic ignored this dig at his apparently dull way of life. He gave Miles a rapid summary of the events of the past few days. At the end of the story, Miles sank back into the leather Chesterfield sofa and whistled loudly through his teeth.

"I withdraw my previous comments. You may not be clubbing, but you're certainly showing some moves, old boy. I'm as intrigued as you are now to meet these two students."

Miles picked up the bottle of Glenfiddich and refreshed Dominic's glass. "But what are you going to do once they've shown you whatever it is they've got? You're going to have to be very careful if you insist on acting like some amateur sleuth. The boys in blue will take a pretty dim view of it if they find out, especially as you're a lawyer."

"I was absolutely ready to tell the police everything until yesterday morning at the police station after the car accident. None of us could understand why Inspector Scott said they'd found no identification on Freedman's body. I definitely saw Christophe put the wallet back in his pocket just before the ambulance arrived."

Miles sat up and grasped Dominic's arm melodramatically. "Tell me again what Inspector Scott asked you just before you left."

"He wanted to know who had made the emergency call."

"And you told him that it was the driver. How do you know it was a real ambulance that turned up?"

Dominic's glass paused midway to his mouth.

"Well, it had a siren and flashing blue lights, and the chaps who jumped out were wearing hospital scrubs and seemed to know what they were doing. I didn't ask for their identity cards. You don't, do you?"

Miles sprang to his feet and began to pace up and down the well-worn Persian carpet beside his desk.

"Let's be paranoid for a second. But let's also give the police the benefit of the doubt and assume that they aren't involved. You say this Freedman character was the hospital assassin. That he was killed, and he had a pass for the Palace of Westminster. What if the accident you saw wasn't an accident? Perhaps someone wanted him done away with. Someone moving in political circles. These bad guys dispatch not only a hit man with a black Range Rover to do the job, but a fake ambulance crew to swiftly remove the body. Probably to make sure he's dead as well."

"Just a moment, Miles. I'll play along with the paranoia bit. But be realistic. When the police get involved, they have to go through the proper procedure. This fake ambulance crew would take the body to a real hospital. Surely the hospital staff or the other ambulance crews would spot the fakes?"

Miles laughed. "Haven't you read newspaper stories about the unqualified surgeons working in our hospitals? Or fake nurses patrolling the wards? I think it would be very easy for an ambulance to bowl up to the emergency room with the victim of a road traffic accident and hand over the body. It's even easier now that the National Health Service is increasingly using private ambulances for emergency calls. By the time the police have made their enquiries at the hospital, the fake ambulance crew has made sure he's dead and removed all forms of identification."

"But surely the police would be able to have the body identified from dental records or possibly fingerprints?"

"My dear Dominic, that all takes time. It's highly likely that they won't have his fingerprints on file. Finding dental records can take several weeks. My theory is that whoever commissioned the hit was expecting the usual delays caused by an overload of work to slow everything down. What they hadn't banked on was you three jokers turning up. By the way, can you remember the number plate of the ambulance?"

Before Dominic could answer, the door burst open, and Gemma appeared in the doorway, panting heavily. A second later a shaven-headed man with the build of a heavyweight boxer appeared behind her. It was Harrison, Miles's clerk. Dominic had met him on several previous visits but still only knew him by his last name. Miles had been to Westminster school, and he retained the habit of addressing many people by their last names only.

"I thought I told you you couldn't just barge in 'ere?" Harrison's stentorian voice betrayed his East London roots. It was never a good idea to pick a fight with Harrison. He turned to Miles. "Beg your pardon, Mr. Torrington. This young lady was askin' to see you and Mr. Delingpole. I told 'er she had to wait downstairs, but she was a bit insistent that she come up straight away...."

Gemma dropped a rucksack on Miles's desk. She was flushed and on the verge of tears. "Mr. Delingpole, please help. A man's been following me all the way from Holborn station. He hung back when I got to Lincoln's Inn, but I'm pretty sure he's waiting for me across the street."

Dominic poured a glass of water for Gemma and gently guided her to a chair. "Why have you come alone? I thought that John was coming?"

"Si seems to be improving slightly, so John wanted to stay behind in case he could get a chance to talk to him. John's managed to hack into Si's laptop—"

Gemma's explanation was cut short by the phone ringing. Miles strode across to his desk and answered it. "Torrington. Yes. Really? Does he say who he is? Hmm. Well, I'll get Harrison to go fetch him. Yes, he's with me now. Oh and Jenny, call main security. Just in case."

Harrison was already on his way down the stairs as Miles hung up the phone. "If it's your tail from the station, then he's downstairs now," said Miles. "Apparently he's a detective from Sussex, and he's very insistent on coming up. Just what is it you've brought here?"

"It's Si's laptop. John found some pretty interesting files on it and wanted Mr. Delingpole to see it as soon as possible—"

"Don't tell me any more," interrupted Miles. "Let me ask questions later rather than you volunteering information. The less you disclose now, the less I am legitimately withholding from our boy in blue when he arrives. Leave this to me." Miles removed the laptop from the rucksack and placed it in the top drawer of his desk.

Harrison returned with the detective, and Dominic immediately stepped forward when he recognized Detective Inspector Scott from the day before.

"What an unexpected pleasure to see you again so soon, Detective Inspector. May I introduce Miles Torrington QC? I understand that you already know Gemma. She tells us you've been tailing her through most of London."

DI Scott's pallid complexion flushed for a moment, and he paused to take stock of the situation. "Mr. Delingpole, I must say I'm bemused to find you here. But it's as well you are. You'll be interested to know what this young lady has been up to."

Gemma opened her mouth to speak, but the inspector interrupted before she could start.

"We have reason to believe that John Fraser and Gemma Young are in possession of evidence pertinent to our investigation into the possible attempted murder of Simon Gregory." He looked at the rucksack on the table. "I believe that Gemma Young has brought it here this afternoon. I do hope that you're not complicit in any of this. Mr. Delingpole? Mr. Torrington?"

Miles stepped forward and stood close to the inspector.

He peered up at him over the top of his reading glasses. "Inspector Scott—"

"—Detective Inspector, sir."

"My apologies. Detective Inspector. Members of our nation's much-admired police force are always welcome in my chambers, even when unannounced and uninvited. However, I am sure that you are aware of the need for due process. I'd rather you went through the proper channels if you're saying that I am somehow complicit in the withholding of evidence from your investigation."

DI Scott was about to speak, but Miles raised his hand to silence him as he continued. "That's a very serious accusation to make of a member of the English legal bar, let alone a Queen's Counsel. If you wish to substantiate it further, I suggest you return with a search warrant. Or you can withdraw that accusation immediately and stop tailing our young friend here. Otherwise I'm sure she'll ask for the assistance of Mr. Delingpole and myself in bringing a harassment charge against your force. It would be an instruction we'd reluctantly have to take."

DI Scott looked from Miles to Dominic and then to the rucksack lying on the table. There was a pause before he responded. He chose his words carefully.

"I don't think you realize the dangerous game these students are playing. By failing to cooperate with us, you may be putting them in even greater danger. Perhaps you may be putting your own life at risk. We have good reason to believe the same people are behind the attempted murder of Simon Gregory and the suspected murder of Peter Freedman in Brighton." DI Scott turned to Dominic. "Yes, Mr. Delingpole, we've identified the victim whose death you witnessed two nights ago."

He walked slowly to the door before turning and

addressing his final remark to Miles Torrington. "I'm confident that you'll make Miss Young fully aware of the penalties for obstructing the police, Mr. Torrington. I suggest that you reconsider your position on this matter too." And with that he left the room.

Miles turned to Gemma. "So, young lady, what exactly do you have in that rucksack?"

17

Jonathan's tall French Le Chameau boots sank deep into the sodden ground as he strode across Glynde Reach on the approach to Decoy Wood. He inhaled the damp December air as he paused to listen to the stillness all around. There was no rustle of leaves. They had long fallen and mulched into the soggy ground. A lone robin eyed him from a branch before resuming its pretty tune.

In this place, away from the noise of Brighton's metropolitan seaside, Jonathan could pause and refresh his mind. Now, it was muddled with a thousand thoughts and emotions. After Dominic had left them at the Grand Hotel on Brighton's seafront, Christophe had wanted to spend the afternoon with Jonathan at his tiny cottage in Lewes.

It was an offer that Jonathan found tempting. But he was too distracted by the break-in at Dominic's apartment. He could not stop worrying about his partner. He made an excuse to Christophe about work and left him at the hotel. Jonathan needed space to think, and to worry about Dominic. That was why he came to Glynde Reach. His special place.

Worrying was something that Jonathan rarely did. Much of his life so far had simply happened to him. He seized opportunities if they appealed, ignored them if they bored him. Never had he refused a challenge because it might scare him. He could not understand people who kept doing the same old thing. "What's the worst that can happen, my dear?" he would ask. It was a simple philosophy and, until now, a successful one.

Then he met Dominic. On a beautiful summer's day at the Glyndebourne Opera House, less than a mile from this spot. He loved opera at Glyndebourne more than anywhere else in the world. It was so quintessentially English. The opera house had been built by a rich Englishman in the 1930s. John Christie's wife was an aspirant soprano and loved to perform. So her husband built her a stage to perform on.

On a wonderful afternoon in July, just over two years ago, Jonathan was with a few friends on the lawns around Glyndebourne, setting up their picnic for the long break at the end of the first act. That was when he first saw Dominic, relaxing with friends on a tartan rug just a few yards away. Jonathan thought him the most beautiful man he had ever seen. He could not take his eyes off him as he joined the line to enter the opera house for a performance of Handel's *Rodelinda*. All through the first act, Jonathan barely looked at the stage. Instead, he scanned the auditorium for a sighting of Dominic.

During the ninety-minute interval, while the audience tucked in to their sumptuous picnic meals on the Glyndebourne lawns, Jonathan wasted no time in making himself known to Dominic.

Perhaps it was love at first sight. Jonathan could only be

certain once he had brought Dominic to Glynde Reach the following weekend.

It was a sort of test. He wanted Dominic to love this special place. He wanted to know that they both loved the breath-taking beauty of nature. As they lay on a dog-eared rug beneath the trees that sultry July day, Jonathan knew then that he had found his spiritual, as well as sexual, partner. This was now their chosen place for walks, for picnics, for escaping the world. They were seldom disturbed by other people, even in the height of summer.

Jonathan continued to stride towards Decoy Wood. He already felt a metaphorical weight lifting from his shoulders. Worrying was the most destructive of activities, in his opinion. Walking, by contrast, was the healthiest.

About a hundred yards to his right, he could see faint movements in the thinning undergrowth. It was highly unusual for anyone to be up here, especially in December. Jonathan slipped his hand into the pocket of his jacket and retrieved the binoculars he always carried with him. In the gloom of the December afternoon, he could see the figure of a man. He was looking away from Jonathan, hunched over a bag. From what Jonathan could vaguely see through his binoculars, the man seemed to be operating some kind of electronic equipment. Even from his back view, Jonathan could clearly see who it was: Steve, the skinhead with the 14-hole Grinder boots who had accompanied John into the Bulldog pub two nights ago.

Jonathan considered creeping up on Steve to catch him unawares. He dismissed the idea quickly as pointlessly furtive. Instead, he strode forward purposefully. His boots stomped through the thickening undergrowth on the outskirt of the wood. As Jonathan drew closer, Steve suddenly turned. With hand gestures he motioned Jonathan to be quiet. Then Steve recognized Jonathan. He beckoned him forward with his right hand, the index finger of his left hand still held to his lips.

As Jonathan drew closer, he could see that Steve was staring at a TV monitor. It was mounted on top of a bag lying on the ground. Jonathan crouched down on his haunches to get a clearer view of the screen. It showed the inside of a nesting box. The eyes of a short-eared owl loomed at the camera. The black-and-white pictures were astonishingly clear, almost as though they came from a night-vision camera.

"So you're a bird watcher," he whispered. "Who'd have thought it?"

"She's in that nesting box up there, see." Steve pointed to a tree over to their left. "I put it there over a month ago. First time a bird's checked it out. Beautiful, isn't she? The short-eared owls have adopted Sussex as their home in the past few years. I love them because they fly in daylight too. It's easier to see their beauty. Chances are, if she starts hunting from there, she's gonna stay."

"Have you got other cameras set up around here?"

Steve sat back on the earthy floor and pulled a tablet computer from his bag. Flicking through several maps on the screen, he enlarged one showing a series of small red pins.

"There's nearly twenty nesting boxes with cameras in them. A couple over towards Mount Caburn by the Lewes Downs. This is one of the latest setups. Solar powered with backup batteries, motion detector, wireless video link, and ten days of recording time. All in a small pack under the floor of the nesting box. I got asked to rig them for Sussex University for a longitudinal survey they've commissioned." Steve looked back at the monitor. "She's beautiful, isn't she?"

he repeated. "It's good when you can mix business with pleasure."

Jonathan was fascinated by the clarity of the images on the video monitor. The owl's plumage and markings showed in great detail. He turned to Steve.

"Business? Who else do you spy on, then?"

"Anyone who pays me, mate. I'm one of the best in the country, though I say it myself. Clients are all sorts. From suspicious wives with time and money on their hands to businessmen wanting a bit of inside knowledge. They get me in. I do the rest. Once it's rigged it's pretty well undetectable, unless you've got some really sophisticated equipment."

"Is this the little business you do for young John, then?"

Steve started to pack away the monitor. "I'm not going to start divulging who my clients are. That's commercial—" His last words were cut off by a well-targeted kick to his right kidney. As he lay winded on the ground, Jonathan leapt on top of him and wrapped his hands around Steve's throat.

"Don't play games with me, sonny, or I'll rip your head off. There's a young student lying in a hospital bed that someone's tried to kill. Twice. Another man's been killed by a supposed car accident. And my partner's place has been done over. I want to know what the hell's going on. So don't choose this moment to get all coy with me."

With Jonathan's full weight on top of him, Steve struggled to breathe. His legs flailed and kicked at the muddy ground as he clutched at Jonathan's hands around his throat. In vain, he fought, but Steve's stamina was no match for Jonathan's strength. Slowly his resistance weakened.

Jonathan looked over at the recording equipment scattered across the ground in the struggle. "In a moment, I'm going to take my hands away. And I promise you. If you try to make a run for it, I'll find all these camera rigs, one by one, and destroy them."

Steve gave one last petulant kick before he lay still. "All right. Get off me. I'm not going anywhere. Just give me a moment to get my breath back."

Jonathan stood; with his legs either side of the panting body. He reached down, and helped Steve into a sitting position. The exhausted man put his head between his knees and breathed deeply.

"What exactly is it that you and John were up to with hidden cameras? Spying on MPs, maybe? Or is it drug company executives? Perhaps it's you who took those photographs that Jay found in Simon's bedroom?"

Steve looked up. He had a surprised expression on his face. "You must think we're real shits if for one moment you thought that we'd spy on Simon. So you've seen the photos he's in, have you? Well, we're not the bastards who took them. Just like you, we're trying to find out who did. And what the fuck Simon was doing there."

"If you're one of the best in the country at this kind of surveillance work, taking photos like those would be child's play to you." Jonathan crouched down and thrust his face close to Steve's. He reached out and held Steve's head firmly in his hands.

"Maybe it was all three of you who had a hand in taking the photos. You, John, and Simon. Let's see if I can piece it together. Simon has some interesting contacts as a result of recruiting drug-testing guinea pigs for Barton Kane. He and his lover, John, organize a little orgy for them. Meanwhile, they recruit you, the voyeur who's an owl obsessive. They get you to rig a few cameras to catch some interesting party photos. Then you've got the blackmail material you can use to make a fistful of money."

Jonathan shoved Steve's face away from him and stood up again. "But it's all backfired on the three of you, hasn't it?"

"No, you've got it all wrong!" Steve scrambled to his feet and leaned heavily against a tree. He breathed deeply. "All right. Listen. I have done rigs for John. But Simon's got nothing to do with them. You've got to believe me, mate. We're on the same side here. Simon's got into something way over his head. We're all trying to find out what it is before anything else happens."

"If you want me to believe you, you're going to have to tell me more about what you and John have been up to. What rigs have you done for him?"

Steve eyed Jonathan warily for several seconds. Then his shoulders sagged in defeat, and he stepped forward to the tablet computer resting on his bag. He flicked through several screens before holding the computer for Jonathan to see. On it was the image of a meeting room in a modern-looking building. A group of five people sat around a table.

"The examination committee. They meet in the biochemistry department at Brighton University. They're deciding on the marking scheme for the end of year exams. John's exams. I did it to show him I could. I did it so he might show a bit more interest in me. But he's besotted with Simon. Not surprising, really. He is very cute."

Jonathan laughed and handed the tablet back to Steve, who put it back on his bag. "That's a hell of a thing to do just for a pickup. I presume you boasted about what you did, and he asked for a little help?"

"No, it wasn't like that. We met at Legends, and when I found out he was struggling with his degree, I thought I'd give him a little help. But he wasn't impressed. Told me he'd rather fail than cheat." Steve shrugged his shoulders. "I just don't understand some people."

"He's an admirable young man," replied Jonathan. "You could learn a thing or two from him about ethics and morals by the sound of it. It strikes me that you move in some pretty dodgy circles with your line of work. How do you sleep at night?"

This time it was Steve's turn to vent his anger. He took a swing at Jonathan's chin with his fist. Jonathan grabbed his arm easily as it flew towards him and twisted it behind Steve's back.

"If you want some rough play, young man, I'm sure we can arrange something. But you've got to work for it first. With your contacts in this shady surveillance business of yours, I'm sure you could find out who rigged the cameras that took those photos. I suggest you and I sit down and think of a way to find them. If you want to impress John, that's the best thing you can do right now."

18

THE MOTORCYCLE courier had been parked in the grounds of Lincoln's Inn for over an hour. The winter chill was beginning to make him shiver, despite the thick Gore-Tex layers he was wearing.

Through the earpieces inside his helmet, he could clearly hear the conversation in Miles Torrington's office fifty yards away. The picture quality of the micro camera secreted in Dominic Delingpole's glasses was less successful.

As he peered at the small video monitor cupped in his gloved hands, the courier adjusted the digital antennae mounted behind him. The only motorcycle parking bay that had been available to him was just on the edge of the reception range for the micro transmitter. As a result, every ten or fifteen seconds the picture on the screen in front of him either broke up or froze. There was no way he could move the bike closer to Miles's offices without drawing attention to himself. His client would have to make do with substandard pictures. At least the sound from the microphones also hidden in Delingpole's glasses was crystal clear. It was even in stereo.

———

DOMINIC WAITED until Harrison and the inspector had left his office. Then he turned to Miles.

"As if I could ever forget why I book you to do my advocacy— that was a good reminder. I don't think he'll be hurrying back here any time soon."

Miles took a short bow before he crossed to his desk and opened the top drawer.

"Please never hesitate to praise me, dear Dominic. You know how I love an appreciative audience. And the judges in court these days are such prissy prigs. You know I have a certain fondness for the older ones. At least they enjoy the sport of the courtroom."

Miles reached into the drawer and retrieved the battered laptop from its hiding place. He put it on the desktop alongside the rucksack in which it had arrived. Dominic felt a frisson of excitement as he wondered what Simon's laptop might reveal.

Miles opened the lid of the computer and turned to Gemma. "Well, young lady. What's all this about?"

Gemma carefully removed the manila envelope of security-camera photographs from the rucksack and placed it alongside the laptop.

"I've brought two things for you to see. Mr. Delingpole has already seen these." Gemma indicated the envelope of security-camera photographs. "And I've also got stuff to show you on Si's laptop. John's managed to hack into it and reckons he's found some major evidence of blackmail. He's found a file of names and contacts, including those of a junior minister in the Department of Health and another Member of Parliament. Despite the things we've discovered about Si in the last few days, we still can't believe he's a blackmailer. So what we think is...."

Miles held up his hand, and Gemma stopped in mid sentence. "I'm forgetting one vital matter. Please don't say any more, young lady." Miles picked up the phone on his desk. "Harrison? Could you pop up with the scanner, please?"

Miles turned to Dominic. "After what our inspector friend said, I think it would be wise to take precautions."

A moment later the door opened, and Miles's clerk entered the room with several pieces of electronic equip- ment in a large sports holdall. Placing headphones on his head and taking a looped wand similar to the one used by security staff at airports, he began moving around the room. As he passed by the Chesterfield where Dominic was sitting, he stopped and shoved the headphones partially from one ear.

"Mr. Delingpole, sir. Would you care to stand up, please?"

Dominic stood, and Harrison slowly passed the detector up the left side of Dominic's body. As he reached Dominic's shoulders, he paused before carefully holding the detector to the side of Dominic's head. After a few moments, he put the detector down on a table and removed the headphones.

"Excuse me, sir, would you be so kind as to remove your glasses and put them on the table?"

While Dominic took off his glasses, Harrison removed another handheld device from the sports holdall and put it on the table alongside Dominic's glasses. After just a few seconds, an image from the camera mounted in the bridge of the glasses appeared on the device's screen.

"Good God, Delingpole, how long have you had those?" Miles strode over to the table and picked up the spectacles. He waved them around in the air to confirm they were the source of the pictures on Harrison's security detector.

Dominic sat back down and stared at the screen. He knew precisely what had happened. The glasses had been in the parcel Gillian gave him when he arrived at his apartment the day before. He had assumed that his optician had sent them. Dominic felt his stomach turn over at the thought that he had been bugged since yesterday when he first put them on. What had he revealed? And more importantly, who was receiving the video?

Harrison took the spectacles from Miles and snapped off one of the arms. Immediately the image on the screen went blank. He carried the glasses over to the window to examine them in the fading afternoon sunlight. "Sophisticated bit of kit, sir. We're not dealing with small-time operators here. Short range, though. Certainly for the video. I'd say the snoopers are nearby."

Dominic and Miles jumped up as a motorbike engine roared into life outside. They crossed the room to join Harrison at the casement window and watched a battered Honda 1300 in the courtyard below. It spun around, sending a plume of black smoke into the air, almost collided with another courier motorbike, and then cut around the security barrier and sped off.

"There he goes," remarked Harrison. "The antenna's mounted on the back. Should have spotted it earlier, but I've been up to my eyes this afternoon. Bit unsubtle of him. We'll have the number plate on the cameras. Though he's probably going to ditch that bike as soon as he can. I'll let Harry down at the City of London Police know, just in case they can catch him for a broken headlight or something."

Harrison drew the blinds and turned to Miles. "The room's clean now, sir, but keep these closed while you're looking at stuff. In case they've got a lens out there."

Harrison handed the detector to Dominic. "Take this. When you get home, check all your rooms. And your car. And be careful what you say on your mobile phone. Best if you switch it off when you're not using it. That way they can't track you."

Then he packed up the rest of his equipment and left the room. Dominic carried the detector over to the Chesterfield sofa and collapsed onto it. He was weary and more than a little dejected over this latest turn of events.

Miles walked across and sat down beside him, putting a comforting arm on his shoulder. "Don't worry old boy. We'll take care of you. Wonderful man, Harrison. Don't know what we'd do without him."

Dominic gave a wan smile to his friend. "I feel like I'm under siege all of a sudden. Just a few days ago, I was nothing more than a provincial lawyer...."

"And you still are, Dominic." Miles leapt up and strode over to the open laptop on his desk. "Don't brood. Best thing we can do is get busy. Now, we'll look at this laptop in a moment. Then we can work out our plan of action. Whoever's behind all this has clearly got money, resources, and connections. We don't know who they may have bought off. That means there aren't too many people we can rely on at the moment." He paused and shook his head chidingly. "Dominic, what have you got me into?"

THE COURIER drove his motorcycle into the underground car park off Parker Mews, a short distance from Lincoln's Inn, killed the engine, and dismounted. Opening one of the panniers, he took out a replacement number plate and a small screwdriver. From the top box he removed a white crash helmet to swap with the black one he was wearing. He put a high visibility vest on over his black Gore-Tex suit. After switching the number plates, he removed the digital antennae and placed the black helmet in the top box. It was the best identity change he could manage in the circumstances. At least when he drove back out again, the police would be less likely to connect him with the bike that had entered the car park.

Then he waited for his client. It had been a frustrating afternoon, and he was unhappy to be delivering sub-standard goods. He could wave good-bye to the balance of his fee, but that was nothing compared to the dent to his reputation. If he had known more about the target's security awareness, he would have used a different surveillance approach.

His musings were cut short by the arrival of a black Mercedes with tinted windows. The car drew alongside him and a door opened.

"Get in." The courier heard a woman's voice from inside the car. He had heard it only once before, when she had called to ask him about his experience in eavesdropping. The voice had a soft Irish accent, edged with authority. "Give me your report."

The courier climbed into the empty rear seat, and the car descended to the next level down in the underground car park. The woman parked but left the engine running.

She switched on the courtesy light and studied her face in the rear-view mirror. Her cheekbones were high and strongly defined, her eyes a vivid emerald green. She reached for a handbag on the passenger seat beside her and pulled out a lipstick. With great care she redefined the edges of her thin lips. She surveyed her handiwork for several seconds, before dropping the lipstick back into the bag. Then she turned and stared directly at the courier in the back of the Mercedes.

"What do you have?"

Although her voice was calm and almost lilting, her left eye twitched involuntarily every few seconds. He tried to avoid staring as he gave his report.

"The bug was discovered. They had scanning. I've got some stuff, but the picture quality's not great. The students have got a laptop belonging to Simon Gregory. We need to get it. My guess is that they'll leave it at the lawyer's offices. But it's going to be tricky, given what the lawyer's people seem to know about surveillance. Perhaps—"

"No matter," the woman interrupted. "Give me what you have." The courier placed the data card in her outstretched gloved hand. They sat in silence for nearly twenty minutes as she reviewed what had been recorded. The pictures flicked past on a small monitor set into the dashboard of the Mercedes. The woman spooled rapidly through some of the material, slowing it from time to time to view sections. Finally she reached the end of the recording.

With the picture frozen on the screen, she sat back for a few minutes, staring out at the dirt spattered concrete wall of the car park.

"Disappointing." The woman began to gather her belongings, not looking at the courier. "But all is not lost. We have a data expert who is working on this. We can find out what those students know. You don't need to do anything further. Wait there for one moment please."

The woman got out of the car and closed her door carefully. The courier watched her walk a short way up the exit ramp. She pulled the fur-lined collar of her black knee-length coat up around her neck. He saw her reach into her pocket and pull out what looked like a mobile phone. Then she stopped and turned to look at him for a few seconds.

Her gaze returned to the device in her hand. She pressed a few buttons. The doors on the Mercedes locked. Somewhere within the ventilation system, there was a faint click and a valve activated. The engine revved to high speed, and exhaust fumes began to enter the passenger compartment.

The courier grabbed the door handle and pulled hard, but it did nothing. He threw himself towards the front of the car and tried the driver's door, but that too was locked. Frantically, he punched at what looked like the central locking controls. None of the controls inside the car seemed to work.

He could feel his throat tighten as the exhaust fumes began to penetrate his airways, and he tried to take shallower breaths. He stretched out on the backseat of the car, bent his legs, and then kicked with full force at the side door. It remained firmly closed, sealing in the poisonous fumes.

Scrambling into the front seat once more, he wrestled with the flaps of the air vents. He was powerless to stop the relentless flow of fumes into the cabin.

THE WOMAN watched the courier's desperate struggles grow weaker as his body succumbed to the poisonous air inside the car. Only the muffled sound of his coughing penetrated the thick glass. It took several minutes until the movements in the car finally stopped.

The woman waited a few moments longer before she walked back to the car. The courier lay slumped on the backseat. She pressed a button on the remote control in her hand. There was the faint click of a valve somewhere inside the car. The engine revved again. This time the ventilation system pumped the exhaust fumes out of the passenger compartment.

Holding her nose delicately with her left hand, the woman unlocked the back door of the Mercedes, and opened it carefully. She reached in tentatively with her right hand and felt for a pulse on the neck of the motionless courier. After several minutes she was satisfied that he was dead. She closed and locked the door and started to walk away, up the exit ramp of the car park. As she did, she reached into her pocket for her mobile phone and made a call.

"A failure, sadly. Although it's likely the target list is out there. I'm returning now. We need to discuss our damage limitation strategy. Could you arrange a clean up operation please? There's one more person I need to deal with here. Let me know when it's done."

She paused for a moment, listening to the voice at the other end.

"No, do nothing with the students for the moment. We may glean more from them through observation. The one in hospital remains a risk. But he has police protection now, so our job is made a little harder. As for the Delingpole man, given our time pressures, perhaps we should use more persuasive methods with him."

19

Samantha had finally succumbed to sleep. The hospital staff had found her a room in the nurses' hostel, and she slept for over five hours. A nightmare finally woke her. A nightmare in which Simon was telling her she had failed as a mother and was the reason he had taken an overdose. Waking in a pool of perspiration, she lay still in the darkness, allowing her racing heart to calm down.

She reached for the small bedside shelf and peered at her mobile phone. It was five in the morning. The hospital day would be starting in less than an hour. Samantha curled up as she used to when she was a child, and pulled the bedclothes tight around her. She would allow herself another five minutes, she decided. Five minutes more in this safe cocoon of warmth.

Half an hour later, showered but still wearing the same clothes from the previous day, Samantha stood outside Simon's room. She watched her son through the window as he slept. The tube in his throat had been removed, and he looked peaceful compared with just a few hours ago. A police officer was on duty by the door. There had been a shift change, and she chatted with the officer for a moment. The senior nurse, who had been checking Simon's monitors, emerged from his room. She turned to Samantha, gently took her hand, and squeezed it comfortingly.

"We think he's turned the corner, love," she whispered. "He's still got a long way to go, but he's off the danger list for the moment. Why don't you pop in and sit with him for a little while? If he wakes up, he won't be able to say much. His throat will be very sore from the intubation." She gently released Samantha's hand. "Then you must get yourself out of the hospital for just a few hours. Young Simon's going to be staying with us for a while yet. Why don't you get some things to busy yourself with in the days ahead? Do you have work to do?"

Samantha shook her head. Following Richard's death, she had received a small insurance payout. When she invested that, together with the proceeds from the sale of the house, it had given her a small independent income to live on. Now she worried whether their first-floor apartment in a creaking Georgian building would be suitable for Simon. What if he was left physically disabled from the overdose? What if she had to pay for long-term care for him? Once again Samantha felt very alone.

She thanked the nurse for her kindness and went into Simon's room. She settled herself in the chair alongside his bed and reached across to gently stroke the fringe of hair lying on his forehead. He stirred, and his eyelids flickered open. His unfocused gaze met her eyes.

"I'm sorry, Mum." Simon's hoarse, almost inaudible whisper caused tears of relief to form in her eyes.

"Don't try to speak for the moment, Simon, darling. They told me that your throat would be very sore." She continued to brush his forehead with her right hand. With her left hand she squeezed his arm gently.

"I've got to speak to John. Tell him to look under my bed. There's a large envelope there. Tell him it's the envelope."

Simon's eyes closed. It seemed that even the effort to speak had been too much for his exhausted body. Then his lips moved one more time. "It's the envelope. Tell him it's the envelope."

———

DOMINIC PEERED through the closed blinds into the dimly lit courtyard below. What he was looking for he had no idea. But knowing he had been bugged left him acutely paranoid. Finally, he left the window and joined Miles at his desk. Together they examined the security camera photographs for several minutes in silence. Miles carefully placed them back on the envelope lying on the desk.

"Fascinating. And you say it's Simon's reflection in the mirror? Well, I'm sure from what you say about his character that he's not blackmailing anyone with these. Perhaps they were planted on him." He took off his glasses and looked across at Gemma. "He's a student journalist? It's very clear, then. He's gathering evidence. But of what? I wonder where those photos were taken? It looks very grand. Oak-panelled. Tudor with bizarre hints of Gothic. Someone with a lot of money likes a steamy time."

Gemma opened the laptop screen again. "John and I went through the list of names and checked out their images on the internet. We can see only two of them in the photos. But they're big names."

She shuffled through the photos and picked one out.

"Look here. In the top right corner of the picture. We're confident that he's Professor Heinz Müller, director of genetic research for Barton Kane."

Gemma picked out a second photograph and turned it to Miles. "And here, on the edge of frame. Not quite so clear because he's in profile. It's Michael Kerrington MP, junior minister at the Department for Health."

Miles replaced his reading glasses and peered at the photograph. "Good God, what on earth is he doing in a gathering like that? He's married. So much to lose." Miles studied the two photographs. "This is interesting. Neither of our big names is actually joining in the sexual jollity. You might question why they were there. But on the basis of these photographs, you couldn't allege they were actually taking part in the proceedings."

Gemma turned the laptop screen around and showed Miles and Dominic a page of close typed text.

"John's been doing a bit of research into Professor Müller from Barton Kane. Müller's been writing papers on genetic manipulation techniques for several years. He researches the techniques behind chemical therapies that could treat identifiable genetic failures."

Dominic's knowledge of medical science was slight, but he was uncomfortable with what Gemma was describing. "Isn't that eugenics, by any other name?"

Miles raised an eyebrow at him. "Dominic, I'm surprised at you. Eugenics is about controlled breeding. It leads ultimately to a dull but pure master race. Gene therapy has the potential to treat diseases. Parkinson's disease, Huntington's disease, cancer. It's an extremely promising area of research for drug companies. And the ones that succeed stand to make millions."

Gemma flicked through a couple of pages on the laptop screen and highlighted a section. "Well, Mr. Torrington, some people might disagree with you on that. Professor Müller works on what's called germ line gene therapy. John gets really excited about it because he says it's got the potential to permanently treat a disease. But it's banned in a few countries because the therapy can permanently modify genes for subsequent generations. In fact its opponents call it a form of eugenics."

Dominic shook his head. "And yet, knowing this, young John is happy to recruit people like Simon to Barton Kane's drug trials?"

Gemma's eyes flashed as she stood to face Dominic. "Yes, he is. And so am I. Without these kinds of drug trials, we'd have no progress in medicine. People are surviving cancer for longer. We're close to having a treatment for cystic fibrosis. Would you like all that to stand still so you can comfort yourself with casting the drug companies as the fat cat bogeymen?"

Miles roared with laughter. "I think this young lady has got the measure of your fine principles, Dominic. Beware your high horse. She seems to have thought about the subject. Her friend John has been researching it. And young Simon too. Besides, a company the size of Barton Kane will have many drug trials operating at any one time. I presume that the chances of the students Simon recruited for them actually being involved in testing genetic therapies are pretty small?"

"Oh no, it's entirely possible, Mr. Torrington," replied Gemma. "But the trials would be strictly controlled by the Gene Therapy Advisory Committee. John's very confident that Barton Kane would only release a drug for human trials once they'd thoroughly tested it in the lab."

Dominic's phone rang. Jonathan's name flashed up on the screen, and he answered the call. "Before you say too much, Jonathan, it seems like someone is spying on us. We can't trust my mobile phone, or yours for that matter."

"Well, lover, I seem to have found a friend who could help us with that. I'll tell you more later. I'm getting into London at Victoria station in just over an hour. Will you be finished in Lincoln's Inn in time to come and meet me?"

Dominic was taken aback by the question. He knew for certain that he had not had time to tell Jonathan about his plans to meet Miles that afternoon.

"How did you know I was here? Did Gillian tell you?"

"No, and after what you've just told me about your phone, I won't explain any more just now. So are you meeting me or not?"

With everything that had been going on, Dominic had forgotten Jonathan was traveling up for the dinner at Chequers that evening. Dominic had been looking forward to the event. But the discovery of the bugged glasses and the encounter with Inspector Scott had unnerved him. At this point a quiet night in with a glass of wine seemed much more appealing.

Dominic sighed. "Let's meet at Marylebone Station for the five o'clock train. That gets us back to my apartment with plenty of time to change and be ready for the car that's picking us up at seven to take us to Chequers."

"A car?" Jonathan said. "Excellent. That means we can both get blind drunk. See you later, lover. Bye."

Dominic had a sudden vision of being thrown out of the prime minister's country residence as a result of Jonathan being let loose on the champagne.

"Chequers, did you say?" Miles picked up one of the photographs and waved it at Dominic. "You do know that the interior of Chequers is oak-panelled? Tudor, possibly? Is it too ridiculous a thought to consider that these shenanigans might have taken place there?"

Dominic was speechless for a moment. It seemed absurd that one of the most secure government buildings in the country could have been the scene of a male orgy. But after all that had happened, anything was possible.

"Miles, I will find out later tonight And if I do find anything, you'll be the first to know. Meanwhile, can Gemma leave this evidence in your safekeeping?"

"Of course. I'll get Harrison to load the contents of the laptop onto our secure server so you can look at the files remotely." Miles quickly wrote logins and passwords on two pieces of paper and handed them to Dominic and Gemma.

"Learn those and then destroy the paper," he said. "I'll get my intern to go through the files with a fine-tooth comb. She did her first degree in mathematics. She got bored with that and has now decided to study for the bar. Amazing person. Brain the size of a planet. I'm sure she'll come up with some interesting stuff."

He turned to Gemma. "You get back to Simon as quickly as you can. Let's hope he continues to improve and that you can speak to him soon. We need to know what he was doing with those photographs and that list of names. The problem is, so do a lot of other people. People with very sinister motives."

20

JONATHAN WAS waiting by the coffee stand when Dominic got to the top of the escalators at Marylebone Station. To Dominic's embarrassment, he rushed over and embraced him.

"Lover, I am so pleased to see you! There's so much to tell!"

"What's he doing here?" hissed Dominic in Jonathan's ear. Out of the corner of his eye, he could see Steve grinning broadly. There was a small pile of bags at his feet.

"Oh, he's going to be the key to solving our little adventure," Jonathan said. "I just know it. Turns out he's an expert in espionage. He's like Q out of James Bond, only far better looking. It was Steve who showed me you were in Lincoln's Inn. He tracked your mobile phone on his laptop. Very accurate it is too. He can also set up surveillance cameras, hack into computers—all that clever stuff. He's coming back with us to check out your apartment and car for bugs or cameras. Given everything that's been happening, I just knew you wouldn't mind."

Dominic had already guessed that Jonathan was

smitten with Steve. He had suspected it from the moment they met John and Steve in the Bulldog pub two nights ago. It had never been easy for Dominic to accept the way Jonathan got distracted by younger men. He found it hard to suppress his instinctive jealousy whenever Jonathan casually described a one-night encounter. Dominic knew that many successful gay partnerships lasted for twenty years or more precisely because they were open relationships. "Sex and love are not the same thing, lover," Jonathan had told him on more than one occasion. "I love you to the end of the world, but we must be free to have other sexual experiences from time to time. It can only make our own relationship stronger."

In the two years they had been together, Dominic had grown to accept what Jonathan described as "open monogamy." He had even experimented with occasional one-night stands himself. But his natural reserve, coupled with his childhood memories of Sunday school and threatening sermons from the vicar had left him feeling awkward and strangely guilty.

It was a constant anxiety he had been unable to shrug off in the two years he had been with Jonathan. He tried to push it to the back of his mind and concentrate on the practicalities of what they had to do. He was not going to solve the mysteries of his relationship with Jonathan just now.

"I suppose after what happened at Miles's chambers today it would be useful if someone who actually knows what they're doing checked the apartment for bugs." Dominic began to explain the events of the afternoon. He took out the scanning device Harrison had given him earlier and showed it to Steve.

Steve examined it, then handed it back. "Hmm, it's all well and good, but it only finds devices that are already operational. I've got a few other toys here that should find dormant devices waiting to be activated."

Jonathan looked triumphantly at Dominic. "There you are. I told you he was essential. And wait until you see his mobile phone tracking thingy. It's so clever. That's settled, then. Steve can check the apartment for bugs and look through the files from Simon Gregory's computer while we're hobnobbing with the great and the good at Chequers."

At that moment their train was announced, and the three men headed for the ticket barriers.

GEMMA SENT John a text as she left the offices in Lincoln's Inn. She wanted to find out if there was any news on Simon's condition. As she made her way to Holborn Station along Kingsway, she kept glancing behind. There was no sign of Detective Inspector Scott or of anyone else tailing her as far as she could see.

She queued with hundreds of other commuters to go through the ticket barriers, then realized that in her haste she had forgotten to buy a ticket. Turning around she collided with a woman wearing a black coat with a fur-lined collar, standing close behind her.

"Oh, I'm so sorry," she said, but the woman said nothing, looked away, and stepped to one side. After Gemma had bought her ticket, she walked through the barriers and took the long escalator leading down to the Central Line. She paused to catch her breath and turned to see the woman in the black coat hurrying down the stairs alongside the escalator.

Pushing her way along the platform Gemma found a clearing in the crowds and stood waiting for the train. She took the rucksack off her back and placed it at her feet. Although it no longer contained the laptop, it still held a few valuables and Gemma wanted to keep a close eye on it in the crowds.

A stale, warm headwind of air announced the approaching train. Gemma reached down for the rucksack in readiness to get on board when the doors opened. But the bag had disappeared. She bent to look on the platform around her feet, but there was no sign of the battered black rucksack.

The roar of the train filled her ears and people shuffled around her into what they hoped would be the optimum position to get on first.

The train was just twenty feet away when Gemma felt a sharp push in the small of her back. Her hands reached out in a futile attempt to stop herself from falling. The train's brakes screeched, a woman screamed, and a man's hand clawed in vain at Gemma's coat, trying to save her as she fell beneath the wheels.

JOHN STOOD with Samantha outside Simon's room. She told him what Simon had said about the envelope.

"He told me to tell you that it's under his bed. It's clearly very important to him. Can you go and bring it back here? Simon might have woken up again by the time you get back, and we can look at it together."

John explained how Gemma had already taken the envelope to London. How he had tried to call Gemma about it, but his mobile phone was dead and needed recharging. Samantha looked irritated.

"So you already knew about the envelope. Why didn't you tell me?"

Now was not the time for Samantha Gregory to know about the photographs they had found in the envelope, John decided. It would only upset her, and as yet, John had no good explanation to offer her.

"Can I sit with Simon for a while?" he asked her. "Perhaps he might wake again soon. I need to ask him some questions to help Gemma and Mr. Delingpole make sense of all this."

Samantha looked at him but said nothing. After what felt like an age, his eyes began to cloud with tears, and he looked away.

"Please, Mrs. Gregory. I can't go back to the house alone again. Not just yet."

Samantha took John's hand in hers and gently squeezed it. "You really do love him, don't you? There's so much I don't know about Simon. Perhaps you can help me to reach him again."

She opened the door of Simon's room and ushered John in. As their chairs scraped on the tiled floor, Simon stirred, and his eyes flickered open.

"John? Is that you?"

John leaned across the bed and held Simon's hand gently. "Yes, it's me. Your mum's let me sit with you for a while. How are you feeling?"

"I don't really feel anything. I can't remember how I got here. I'm just incredibly sleepy...." His voice tailed off, and his eyes slowly closed.

John leaned close to Simon's ear and whispered, "I love you so much. Don't leave me now."

Simon's eyes flickered open again. "You're soft in the head, you are. Falling for an idiot like me. I thought I was the big investigative journalist. But it seems I've made a bit of a mess of everything." He squeezed John's hand. "I'm so glad you're here. You can help me sort it out now. Did Mum tell you about the envelope?"

John nodded. "We've seen the photographs and worked out who a few of the people are. What on earth were you doing at something like that?"

Simon slowly turned his head from side to side on the pillow. "It's not the photographs. They're not important. I was just keeping them as a bit of insurance. It's the envelope itself. You've got to look inside. At the bottom. Hidden away. There's a data card taped deep inside it. Look for the data card. It's got the transactions. They're the real evidence." Simon's eyes closed and he drifted back to sleep.

———————

DOMINIC PEERED over Steve's shoulder to try to see the monitor screen he was holding. Steve pointed it at different parts of Dominic's living room; Dominic could just see some kind of calibration grid on the small screen. Two small red dots pulsed, and a map representing the layout of his room appeared.

Jonathan appeared at his side.

"It's jolly clever, isn't it, dear thing? As I said at Marylebone Station, Steve is our Q to your double o seven. You just need a martini in your hand and the illusion is complete."

Steve set the monitor down on the coffee table and walked over to the mirror above the fireplace.

"Can we take this mirror down, Mr. Delingpole? I need to examine it."

Jonathan and Dominic carefully lifted the large mirror

off its hangings and rested it on the carpet. The thin black package attached to its back was immediately visible.

"Clever," Steve remarked. "Microphone and wide-angle lens of the room. Movement and sound activated. Transmits to the phone line by the looks of it." He picked up the telephone base unit, which sat on the bookshelf to the side of the fireplace. "Yes, here's the receiver. There'll be other devices in the apartment, all sending to this. Neat."

Dominic thought it was anything but neat. He felt violated. He watched as Steve moved to the window and reached up to the pelmet above the curtain. A moment later Steve removed another thin black package, similar to the one he'd found on the back of the mirror.

"That's this room clear. I'll start on the kitchen now." Steve picked up his monitoring equipment and left the room.

Dominic sat down on the settee and turned to Jonathan. "Do you know how horrible this feels? A few days ago, this was my home. My sanctuary from the world. Now it feels like a goldfish bowl. And what if they've done your cottage as well? We're not private anywhere all of a sudden."

Jonathan sat on the settee beside Dominic and put an arm around his shoulders. "Steve's already checked out the cottage, and it's clear. He's also rigged an alarm so we'll know if anyone tries to break in. He'll do the same here. Come on, lover. Give me a hug. Then let's get ready for our big night out. Life must keep going as normal. Now," he paused and looked mischievously at Dominic. "I've brought my dress kilt especially for tonight. As it's the prime minister's country residence, should I wear anything underneath? Or can I let the breeze blow free?"

21

Jonathan decided he looked particularly glamorous in his blue-and-green tartan dress kilt. He poured two glasses of prosecco and waited for his partner to be ready. Earlier, Dominic had announced that he refused go into the bathroom until Steve could confirm it was clear of bugging devices. Jonathan had no concerns about being seen naked on a hidden camera. He jumped into the shower first, while Steve scanned the room for bugs. As he stood drying himself with the towel, Jonathan teasingly called Dominic to join him and explore the exhibitionist side of his personality. Dominic declined the invitation.

Eventually, wearing his Paul Smith dinner jacket over a white wing-collar shirt, Dominic joined Jonathan in the living room and handed over his bowtie.

"Would you tie it for me, please, love? Your Glyndebourne experience means you do it so much better than me."

Jonathan kissed him on the lips. "Flattery will get you everywhere, lover." He picked up the two glasses of prosecco. "Let's first drink a toast to our idiotic prime minister.

The person who has so decently invited us to their country mansion." He handed a glass to Dominic and clinked them together. "Cheers, my dear. Let's see if I can drink them all under the table tonight."

Dominic took a sip of his prosecco. "Hmm, as soon as we arrive, I'm going to announce that you're dangerously allergic to alcohol, and you must be confined to orange juice for the whole evening."

"Probably not a million miles from the truth." Jonathan set down his glass and began to tie Dominic's bowtie. "Why haven't you been to Chequers before, seeing as it's only thirty minutes down the road?"

"Well, you do have to be invited by whoever's prime minister at the time," replied Dominic. "But I have rambled through the grounds many times. It's a very pleasant walk."

Jonathan enjoyed dressing his partner, who, he felt, did not pay enough attention to how he looked. Detail was everything.

"How on earth can you walk through the grounds? Surely it's completely locked down with security fences and barbed wire?" Jonathan flattened the butterfly wings of the completed bowtie and admired his handiwork.

"There's actually a public footpath that runs right across the grounds of Chequers," Dominic explained. "It's not far from the gatehouse. Of course the path is surrounded by cameras and bollards. A previous prime minister, I think it was Tony Blair, tried to get the footpath closed. But the Ramblers' Association successfully opposed him. Quite right too. Our rights to roam must be protected."

Jonathan began to slide his hands down the front of Dominic's jacket. "Oh, we all need the right to roam, don't we?" He pulled Dominic close to him.

Dominic responded by leaning forward and kissing him. "Thank you, Jonathan. You've made this possible."

Jonathan took a step back and looked quizzically at his partner. "What on earth do you mean? It's you, not me, who got the invitation for this gig tonight. That came courtesy of your chums on the chamber of commerce."

"No." Dominic held Jonathan's hands to his side. "Tonight is much more than just a bit of a do at Chequers. This is the first time since we met that you'll be my partner in public here in Oxfordshire."

He let go of Jonathan's hands so he could pass him his drink. "I propose a toast. To you, my dear friend and lover. I think it's taken me a bit too long to be honest in public about who I am. You've made tonight possible."

"Well, thank you, my dear. This evening's going to be a riot, isn't it?" Jonathan grinned.

Dominic set his glass down on the coffee table with a sudden crash. "Oh my God. I forgot to tell you something Miles said earlier. When he was looking at those photographs Gemma had brought along, he asked if I had any idea where they had been taken. Do you remember when we looked at them together? The room looked very grand, oak-panelled—"

"I'm afraid I didn't notice the room very much," said Jonathan with a grin, "There was far too much activity in the foreground."

Dominic ignored the interruption. "Miles said it looked Tudor, with a hint of Gothic. Just as I was leaving, he said Chequers is the same style of architecture. I believe he thinks—"

"He thinks Chequers hosted a male orgy?" Jonathan put down his glass and clasped his hands to the waistband of his kilt. "Well, if it did, then I'm pleased I made the right choice to let the breeze blow free tonight."

———

A WHITE Lexus limousine arrived promptly at seven. As Dominic walked out into the hallway of Ash House with Jonathan at his side, a clatter of feet on the stairs announced the arrival of Randolph James from his first-floor apartment.

"Mr. Delingpole! You're looking very smart. Are you going to this shindig at Chequers too? Do you need a ride? My car's just arrived."

"Good evening, Mr. James," Dominic replied. "Thank you for the offer, but we've already got a car. We'll see you there. Let me introduce you to my partner, Jonathan McFadden. Jonathan, this is Randolph James. He's an MP for somewhere up in Yorkshire."

Randolph James shook Jonathan's hand enthusiastically. "Partner, eh? How very modern. And are you a true Scotsman, or is the kilt simply the new fashion?"

Jonathan looked at the MP coldly. "My name's McFadden. And this is my clan's tartan. Its fashion is timeless, Mr. James."

As he and Dominic walked out of Ash House to their waiting limousine, Jonathan said the single word "asshole." But as soon as he caught sight of the chauffeur holding the car door open for them, he visibly brightened. The man was in his early twenties, tall and muscular. He wore black chinos and a contour-hugging black T-shirt.

"Well, hello, young man, you're a sight for sore eyes. And what's your name?"

"I'm Pat, sir."

"Mmm. I'm going to call you Pat the Pecs this evening. I

do hope you've kept your engine running for us. It's a chilly evening, especially when you're wearing a kilt." Jonathan gave the chauffeur a broad wink before climbing into the back of the car.

Dominic smiled. He had met Pat at the gym six months ago. When he had found out Pat was a part-time chauffeur, Dominic had booked him for tonight especially for Jonathan's benefit. And, he supposed, for his own appreciation too.

In a little less than thirty minutes, as the car rounded a final bend in the narrow country road, the gates of Chequers appeared straight ahead of them. Pat the Pecs pulled up alongside the brick gatehouse. Jonathan opened his window to hand their invitations to the security guard as he was sitting on the side closest to the checkpoint.

"Jonathan McFadden and Dominic Delingpole?" the guard asked. "Do you have some photo ID with you, please?" Jonathan handed over his driver's licence.

Patting his chest, Dominic cursed under his breath. "Oh my God, Jonathan. I haven't got my licence. I forgot to transfer my wallet to this jacket! Pat, could you take us back to the apartment please. God, I'm such an idiot."

The chauffeur put the car into reverse gear but they didn't move. Dominic looked over his shoulder and saw that they were blocked by another car immediately behind them. A moment later he heard a familiar voice at the window.

"Mr. Delingpole, is something wrong?" It was Randolph James. His car had been following theirs all the way from Ash House. In the dim interior lighting of their limousine, Dominic saw Jonathan roll his eyes.

"Mr. James, I rather foolishly left my driver's licence back at home, and I can't get in without it. Could you ask your driver to reverse, please, so we can go back and get it?"

"Well, actually, I've just realized I've got to go back and get something as well. A fellow MP from the party is expected to be there, and I've been promising her a document I have in my possession. My driver can run us both back now while your, er, partner goes and joins the merry throng."

Dominic looked across to Jonathan, who simply rolled his eyes again.

"I won't be long, Jonathan. Don't drink everything while I'm away." Dominic got out of the limousine and walked towards the black Mercedes with tinted windows waiting behind.

It was past seven o'clock when John got back to the house. He was desperate to ring Gemma and tell her the new information about the data card he had learned from Simon. But his dead mobile phone meant he could do nothing until he got it back to its charger.

John pushed open the front door and ran up the stairs two at a time. After plugging in the charger, he waited a few minutes until the phone restarted. Then he called Gemma several times. Each time it diverted to her voice mail. On the second attempt, he left her a message.

"Gemma, it's me, John. Call me as soon as you get this message. I've spoken to Si."

Hanging up the call, John thought for a moment, and then he called Steve.

"John. Where the fuck are you?"

"I'm back in the house. Look, I've spoken to Si and...."

"Don't say any more. Go outside. I'll call you back in two minutes."

"I don't think I've got enough battery life for that, Steve. It's pretty dead."

There was a pause at the other end.

"Okay. Hang up and I'll send you a text. When you open it, you'll find it restarts the phone. Then your mobile will be in encrypt mode. Reply with a text with the info in it. Don't talk in the house. Things are getting hot." The line went dead.

Within thirty seconds of the call ending, a text came through from Steve. As John opened it, the screen went dead for a moment before his phone restarted.

John rapidly texted Steve what Simon had told him about the data card and how it was the real evidence. A moment later Steve's reply came back:

Get out of the house now. It's not safe. Go to the hospital and surround yourself with people. Check in with me every ten minutes. All text messages are now encrypted.

John stared at the message, wondering if Steve was playing a joke on him. From downstairs came the sound of glass breaking and the front door being smashed in. John knew then that Steve was deadly serious.

22

STEVE HAD positioned himself by the partially open French windows of Dominic's apartment. The living room lamps were switched off, but the garden lights illuminated the area immediately around the patio. He had also rigged a makeshift set of spotlights shining out into the garden. Meanwhile he had fitted motion sensors on the front door and windows. There were two more sensors placed on the lawn beyond the patio.

A laptop screen was open in front of him. It showed three pulsing red lights accurately indicating the position of the mobile phones belonging to Jonathan, Dominic, and John. Steve had been unable to raise any signal from Gemma's phone. He hoped John's mobile would hold its charge for as long as it took him to get to the Royal Sussex Hospital.

Steve was unnerved by the number of bugging devices he had found in Dominic's apartment. He was acutely aware of the sophistication of whoever had planted the devices. It made him feel out of his depth. He pushed the concerns to the back of his mind as he concentrated on the job in hand.

There had been no answer from Dominic's mobile phone when Steve tried to call him with John's information. It took Steve only a few moments to hack into the calendar on Dominic's phone to find the name of Miles Torrington. Another few minutes' search through the contacts yielded Miles's phone number.

"Mr. Torrington. This is Steve Brown. I'm looking after Dominic's security systems."

"Brown? Ah yes, the young skinhead surveillance chappie. Dominic mentioned you. What is it?"

Steve decided he had been called worse in his time. "Can you hang up and take your mobile phone outside? I need to switch us to an encrypted call. Call me back on this number showing in your phone."

The line went dead. But within a few minutes Steve's phone rang.

"You're an impressive young man," came Miles's voice. "Right. I'm standing in the street outside my apartment. Are we encrypted?"

"Yes, I know you're outside." Steve lost no opportunity to show off his skills with tracking technology. "You're in Silk Street by the Barbican. Do you live in one of those swanky apartments? Must have cost a bomb."

As he was talking, he pulled up a street view of the London Barbican arts complex on his screen. If he had a bit more time, he reckoned he could hack into the security cameras to see exactly where Miles was standing.

"Look, young man." Miles sounded unnerved. "Your technical skills are impressive but would you stop showing off and concentrate on the matter in hand? What is it you want?"

Steve rapidly described what Simon had said about the data card hidden in the envelope of photographs.

"So, young Steve. It seems it's more than just a file of names on Simon's computer that's important. This is getting more and more intriguing. I need to get back to my office and find that data card. I'll call my brilliant pupil back in and get her onto it. Although knowing how keen she is, I bet she'll still be there. I'll call you if I find anything."

Miles ended the call.

JOHN STUFFED his phone and its charger into his jacket pocket and struggled with the old casement window until it suddenly slid up. He heard the front door slam open and was glad that in his haste to get upstairs, he had forgotten to turn any lights on in the house.

Clambering out onto the sill, he pulled the window back down and lowered himself onto the flat roof of the kitchen extension immediately below. He jumped to the ground and ran to the back gate that opened onto the path linking the row of Victorian terraced houses.

Instead of following the path along the route that eventually led back to the road at the front of the house, he jumped a fence into the garden of one of the houses behind. He knew this house had a narrow passageway opening onto a road that led towards Kemp Town. To his relief a noisy group of students were walking past. John joined them, trailing slightly behind. Pulling his hood up around his head and shoving his hands deep into his jacket pocket, he followed them onto Freshfield Road. The group headed south towards the seafront. It would be a brisk fifteen-minute walk to the hospital.

After a little over ten minutes, he came to a pub and ducked inside. He pulled out his phone and was relieved to see it still had some battery life. He sent a text reading simply *OK* to Steve and then cautiously stepped back outside. As he looked up and down the road, he realized he had no idea what he should be looking for. Nor did he know if the person or persons who broke into the house were chasing him. He did know he had never felt so terrified or alone.

About a hundred yards behind him, pulled into the side of the road with its lights still on and the engine running, was a black van. Was it following him? John considered going back inside the pub. But he had to get to the hospital. Staying there only delayed the inevitable.

At that moment, another group of students left the pub and started walking down Freshfield Road. John stepped in behind them and followed closely. After a moment, he turned to look behind him. He could see that the black van was pulling out into the stream of traffic.

IN THE shadowy interior of the black Mercedes, Randolph James's teeth flashed white as he smiled and patted Dominic's arm. "It's rather fortunate that we were just behind you, Mr. Delingpole. I've been wanting to have a little discussion ever since that unfortunate break-in." He leaned forward and murmured something to the driver. A moment later the car turned off onto a side road. It accelerated rapidly and swayed from side to side as the driver expertly navigated the twisting narrow lane.

"I need to drop by the house of one of my constituents. It won't take us long. Which reminds me. I think you may have acquired an envelope recently. An envelope containing some photographs. Could you tell me where it is?" The teeth continued to flash in the darkness, and Dominic felt a chill run down his back.

"Mr. James, could you just take me to Ash House as you promised? I really don't want to keep Jonathan waiting too long."

"Ah yes, the 'partner' you introduced me to. I'm sure the prime minister's household staff will look after him well. And we don't have to be long, provided you can give me that information."

"Are you threatening me, Mr. James?"

"Consider it an opening move in our negotiation. That envelope is part of an on-going investigation, and we don't want the wrong sort of people getting hold of it."

"Then perhaps it should be handed over to the police."

Randolph James leaned in close to Dominic. "So you do have it?" The car braked suddenly and turned left through a gateway onto a gravelled drive. Ahead of them Dominic could see an ivy-clad Gothic-style building. Behind them the gates slowly swung shut. The car pulled up in front of two large oak doors that were the entrance to the house. The driver got out and held the car door open. Randolph James gripped Dominic's arm. A little tighter this time.

"Please join us, Mr. Delingpole. There's someone you should meet."

JONATHAN TWIDDLED the champagne-flute stem between his thumb and index finger. A dribble of liquid lay in the bottom of the glass. He had already refused three offers of a top-up. He was acutely aware of Dominic's concerns for his drinking at such an important event. But nearly an hour had gone by since they parted at the gatehouse, and Jonathan was getting very bored. So far he had endured a long explanation of the benefits of seamless welding from the director of a local engineering firm and some frank opinions on the threat of increasing immigration to British society from an overbearing woman who actually had tints of blue rinse in her hair.

He moved to a corner of the room, took out his mobile phone from his sporran, and called Dominic. There was no answer. Puzzled, he was about to call Steve when he noticed a guest taking a close interest in his Highland outfit.

"Forgive me," said the man, "but what is the significance of the little dagger on your leg? Is it functional, and should I be worried? Or is it merely decorative like a brooch?"

The man could not have been much more than five feet four. He sported a neatly clipped moustache and was peering intently at Jonathan. The man's silver hair was immaculately swept back, and his eyes twinkled behind his small, round gold-rimmed glasses.

"This is called the *sgian dubh*," Jonathan said, embarking on a lecture he always enjoyed. "Its origin is in the seventeenth and eighteenth centuries. Then it was called the *sgian-achlais* and was carried concealed in the armpit. When you entered the house of friends, you'd reveal it by putting it in the top of your stocking. That's the stocking on your right leg so that it's ready for immediate use. Unless you're left-handed. Now please excuse me, I'm worried about a friend of mine and need to make another phone call."

He turned away from the guest and called Steve.

"Has Dominic got there yet? I'm standing around like the last sad lemon on the fruit stall. If he doesn't come back soon I may have to pick up one of these rather lovely waiters."

"I thought Dominic was with you? Why should he be here?"

Jonathan gripped the phone a little tighter.

"He forgot his driver's licence, so he went back with the ghastly politician man from the apartment upstairs to get it. You don't think they've had an accident, do you?"

"His phone's still sending a strong tracker signal," Steve replied. "It looks like he's about two miles from here. Stationary. Let me get a more accurate reference."

There was a pause, presumably while Steve pulled up a detailed map on the screen. Jonathan's hand began to perspire, and he gripped the telephone handset ever tighter.

"I'm pretty sure he's in a place called The Manor off Bragnall Lane. Do you want me to get out there?"

Jonathan took a deep breath. "I think we're finally out of our depth. Adrift in the ocean and without a lifeboat. Neither of us have any idea why Dominic's at this Manor place. And he's not picking up his phone for us to ask him the question. If we go out there on our own, we could end up dead. Dominic might be dead already, for all we know."

He thought for a moment. "Right. We need the place surrounded. Preferably by men with guns. Big guns. What are your connections like with the armed response unit at Thames Valley Police?"

Steve laughed. "You must be kidding. I do security-camera installations. I'm not fucking Jason Bourne."

"Well, use your imagination. Make up a story. Call emergency. Tell them you're at The Manor. That you've taken your family hostage, and you're going to shoot them one by one unless they pay you a million pounds. That should get them out. Meanwhile, I'll get our gorgeous-looking chauffeur to drive me back to Ash House to pick you up. Then he can drive us both over to watch the show at the Manor."

"You're fucking priceless, you are," was all that Steve could say before he ended the call.

Jonathan turned to leave the room and, with irritation, saw that the little man was still standing behind him, apparently listening in.

"You know that's very rude of you," said Jonathan testily. "Why can't you go and mingle with the other dull people here, Mr....?"

"Professor," corrected the small, neat man. "I am Professor Heinz Müller. My company is Barton Kane. You may have heard of us?"

23

"ALLOW ME to introduce Janet Downpatrick. Janet is a very successful investment banker. She's also a founding member of the Natural Family Association. Why don't you sit down, Mr. Delingpole?"

The smile on Randolph James's face seemed to have been created by a plastic surgeon. By contrast, the woman standing by the fireplace in the oak-panelled drawing room of the Manor glowered at Dominic with the contempt of a boarding school headmistress. She was slender and nearly as tall as Dominic. Her auburn hair was scraped back severely into a neat bun. She wore a black trouser suit with black court shoes.

"Why am I here? Are you intending to hold me against my wishes?"

"Sit down, Delingpole." The woman's voice was quiet, with the hint of an Irish accent. But there was no mistaking its authority. "You may be here for some considerable time. If you don't hand back that envelope, we'll start taking actions against your accomplices until you do." She walked up to Dominic and stared at him.

"We may start with your gardening man, McFadden. We have him under surveillance at Chequers. Or we could begin with the student, Fraser. We can easily get him picked up in Brighton. We have connections there, you know. You've already seen what happened to the boy Simon Gregory. We're very persuasive when under duress."

Dominic sat down heavily on the leather Chesterfield sofa facing the fireplace. There was a cramping sickness in the pit of his stomach.

"Randolph James. An elected Member of Parliament." Dominic looked up at the MP. "And you're acting like a common kidnapper. What the hell do you think you're doing?"

Janet Downpatrick cut in before Randolph James could open his mouth.

"You'll find that members of the Natural Family Association hold posts in the highest levels of many organizations around the world. Including governments. We're an international network. We've had some setbacks in Europe in recent years, but we're correcting that now. Tell me, where is that envelope?"

Dominic recalled where he had heard about the Natural Family Association before. Jonathan once told him how the group had disrupted an equal marriage demonstration he attended. They had both dismissed the Association as a bunch of anti-gay cranks.

Janet Downpatrick took out her mobile phone and searched for a number. "Very well, we can begin with McFadden. I believe he's the 'special friend' of yours."

"No, wait. Wait." Dominic desperately wanted to buy some time. He would work out what he could do with that time later.

"The envelope's in a safe in central London. I don't have access to it."

"Thank you for confirming that. It's in the offices of that lawyer you saw earlier today, presumably?" Dominic nodded.

"Then it should be easy enough to recover." Janet Down-patrick leaned close to Dominic, her face just a few inches from his. "You'll come with us into London. Our driver and head of security will hold you in the car while Randolph and I retrieve the document. If it's not in the safe as you claim, there'll be consequences."

Dominic hardly heard her last threat as he stared at the mirror above the fireplace, realizing where he had seen it before. This was the room in which the orgy photographs had been taken.

FOR ONE of the few times in his life, Jonathan was rendered speechless. The short silver-haired man in front of him continued his monologue.

"I'm a research scientist with Barton Kane. We've recently opened a new laboratory not far from here. As a result, I now have the great pleasure of living and working in this delightful part of the world. What is it that you do, Mr. ...?"

"McFadden." Jonathan was racking his brains to remember what Dominic had told him about Barton Kane. "I'm an opera singer at Glyndebourne. Have you ever been?"

Professor Müller tapped the tips of his fingers together with delight. "Earlier this year, for the first time. We saw the revival of Handel's *Rodelinda*. It was charming. So, Mr. McFadden, will I have seen you on the stage?"

"I played Flavio," lied Jonathan, "and I was understudy for Garibaldo. What do you research, Professor? Are you going to be able to finally cure the common cold?"

Professor Müller chuckled and patted Jonathan's arm.

"My dear boy, I'm working on a far more important cure than that. My field is gene therapy. You know, we are very close to being able to correct some of nature's tiresome anomalies. Forever. It all comes down to genes, you see. How short or tall you are, your susceptibility to disease. And of course your sexual orientation."

Jonathan tensed. "Tell me more, Professor. I'm intrigued."

"Oh, it's a fascinating field. It will be possible to remove so many of life's unhappinesses permanently. Terrible diseases like cancer or cystic fibrosis. People will be able to be more normal."

"What do you mean by normal, exactly, Professor?" asked Jonathan suspiciously. "After all, it's our differences that make us interesting."

"Maybe interesting from a scientific or anthropological point of view, Mr. McFadden. But few people are happy at being different. They would much prefer to be normal. I myself would have preferred to be a little taller. I am sure you have found being tall is an advantage on many occasions." Professor Müller puffed out his chest and stood to attention. "I could never have been an opera singer at only five foot five."

"Well, Mario Lanza wasn't much taller than you, and he did quite well. So instead you're a scientist and clearly a very successful one. Isn't it more important for people to make the most of what they've got rather than fooling around with nature? Why try to be something we're not?"

Jonathan waved away the offer of a top-up from a

passing waiter. He was anxious to get away to find Dominic, but at the same time, he could not resist the temptation to stay to demolish the pompous professor.

"I can assure you, Mr. McFadden, we do not 'fool around,' as you call it, in our research. There are many people in this world who are unhappy with being different. Who are you to deny them the opportunity to be more normal if they can? Look at homosexuals for example."

Jonathan was in danger of crushing the champagne glass in his hand.

"They may use the word *gay*, wear flamboyant clothing, and march in the streets saying they're proud. But the reality is that many of them are deeply unhappy. Why? Because they're not normal. People are happiest when they are part of an accepted, normal group in society. When they feel they belong. It will only be a short while now before we can help homosexuals to be normal permanently. It's very exciting. We've already begun trials on a new gene therapy."

Jonathan had heard enough.

"Professor, I've actually got to be somewhere else now. And after what I've just heard, I'm bloody glad I do. Just so as you know, I'm gay, I'm proud, and I'm very happy."

He put down his glass and turned to leave. "You do know that Handel, the composer of Rodelinda, was gay, don't you? And by all accounts he was pretty fucking happy too."

———

WHEN JOHN saw the van pull into the stream of traffic, he pushed past the group of students he had been walking with and broke into a run. He pulled his hooded jacket tightly around him against the December cold. It was only a couple more minutes before he would reach the hospital. His feet beat out a rapid, steady rhythm on the pavement, and his fingers tightened around the mobile phone in his pocket. He comforted himself with the thought that very soon he would be in the warm and could check in with Steve before going to see Simon.

From behind him, the sound of footsteps rapidly approaching set John sprinting for the distant lights of the hospital. His heart was thumping. Despite the cold wind, sweat had broken out on his forehead. He was certain his pursuer was getting closer.

The pounding of feet was drowned out by the roar of an engine and a screech of rubber on the road. The black van he had seen earlier overtook him and pulled in sharply at a road junction ahead. The side door slammed open, and a man wearing a ski mask jumped out. John swerved to the left to avoid him. The hooded man lunged forward and grabbed John's neck, pulling him down into a headlock.

John flailed his fists, desperately trying to do his assailant some injury. He managed to get one punch to his groin. With a howl, the man briefly loosened his grip. As John tried to wriggle free, the man brought his knee up hard into John's face. Then he tightened his headlock again. John could taste blood in his mouth, and his nose was throbbing with pain. Despite his struggles, he was rapidly being overpowered by the sheer bulk of the man. He felt himself being dragged back to the van.

"Oh no you don't!" a familiar Australian voice yelled out from behind him. John was thrown sideways as a body hurled itself at them. The man released his grip, and John rolled to the ground as Jay leapt on top of the man.

"Run, mate, get the fuck out of here!" John's housemate laid punches into his attacker's head. As John scrambled to his feet, the driver's door of the van opened. John leapt around the front of it and slammed the door against the driver's hand, eliciting a howl of pain. Taking a solid grip on the door handle, John then yanked it open, slammed it again, and heard another satisfying yell.

He looked over at Jay, who by this time was standing over the motionless body of the attacker. John was gratified to see a look of approval on his housemate's face.

"Not bad for a poofter, mate. Come on. Let's get to the hospital before the police arrive. I don't think we're going back to the house for a while."

24

THE WEBBING of the seat belt was tight around Dominic's body. Janet Downpatrick sat alongside him in the back of the black Mercedes. She watched with mild amusement as Dominic shifted awkwardly, trying to ease his discomfort.

"You'll find that you're very secure, Mr. Delingpole." She touched a button on the panel to her side and the seat belt tightened further. "And if the belt's a little loose, I can always adjust it for you. It's probably best that you simply keep still."

The Mercedes pulled out of the gateway of The Manor, and the journey to London began. The combined smells of warm leather, Downpatrick's expensive perfume, and the driver's stale sweat, clawed at Dominic's nostrils.

Randolph James sat in the passenger seat in front of Dominic. He turned around with a fixed smile on his face. "Yes, my dear chap. Just sit there quietly. You'll be more comfortable that way." The MP settled back into his seat.

With difficulty, Dominic shifted his body to turn it away from the Downpatrick woman. He needed to avoid her seeing what he was going to do next. Lifting his left hand slowly, he reached into the pocket of his jacket and fumbled for his mobile phone. He found the small switch on its side, and with his thumb, flicked it in the pattern Steve had shown him earlier that evening. He could not risk looking at the phone to confirm he had activated the transmitter. Slowly he dropped his arm back to his side and faced the front. Out of the corner of his eye, he could see Downpatrick watching him in the half-light of the car.

STEVE WAS preparing to clear away his equipment when his laptop beeped with the alert from Dominic's mobile. He sat down at the keyboard and set the audio recorder running. The slightly muffled sound of the interior of the black Mercedes came through the laptop's speakers.

"So you're taking me to Miles's chambers in Lincoln's Inn? How, precisely, do you think you'll get into the safe? Miles has very good security, you know."

Steve listened intently. At the same time, he sent a text message to Jonathan. He needed him back with the car. Quickly.

A woman's voice came through the speakers. "It will be very straightforward. Viktor is not just an excellent driver. He also has many talents when it comes to matters of security. It won't take him very long. You must hope for your sake that the envelope is still there."

"And what do you propose to do with me once you have it? I presume you don't want me to tell the world that Randolph James MP and Janet Downpatrick of the Natural Family Association, whatever that is, are in the kidnapping business."

"The world won't believe you, old chap" came the voice

of Randolph James. "We have connections at the highest level. In every organization. No one's going to believe a preposterous conspiracy story from a tin-pot country lawyer."

"What exactly is this Natural Family Association anyway?" asked Dominic. "Judging from the photos in that envelope, you seem to have an unhealthy interest in male pornography."

Steve began packing the rest of his equipment away in readiness for Jonathan's arrival. He turned up the volume on the laptop, and the soft Irish lilt of the voice he now knew to be that of Janet Downpatrick filled the living room.

"Quite the opposite, Delingpole. We want to put an end to the filth that your sort peddle. Children need families that are natural. Marriage should always be the union of one man and one woman. We'll reverse this recent fashion for the unnatural marriages of homosexuals and lesbians that a minority of governments have approved."

"So you're campaigning against equal marriage? I still don't see why you organize male orgies at The Manor. That's where those photos were taken, isn't it? I recognized the room immediately."

The living room door in Dominic's apartment swung open and Jonathan bounded in. Steve motioned to him to be quiet as they heard the voice of Randolph James.

"Oh, my dear fellow. That was just an amusing sideshow for those who are funding us. You see, we're working to stamp out homosexuality permanently. Thanks to advances in gene therapy, we're very close to repairing the damaged gene that people like you have. Our research partners are already testing the treatment. We host those little parties at the Manor from time to time to see how well the guinea pigs respond to the treatment."

"My God," whispered Jonathan, "I've just met the bastard who's behind all that. Let's get after Dominic. Pat the Pecs has got the engine running downstairs."

IT WAS shortly before ten o'clock when Miles arrived at Lincoln's Inn. His clerk, Harrison, was waiting for him in the reception of his chambers.

"Evenin', Mr. Torrington. I've got the materials from the secure room. They're on your desk. Would you like some coffee, sir?"

"Good man, Harrison. Yes, strong and black is the order of the night, I think. We may be in for a long evening."

Miles entered his office. He picked up the envelope and was examining it closely when his mobile phone rang.

"Mr. Torrington, this is Steve here, the... er, skinhead surveillance chappie."

Miles laughed.

"Perfect timing, dear chap. I'm in my chambers now and just about to open the envelope."

"Well, don't. Dominic's been kidnapped. He's in a car with some creeps heading for your office. They're after the envelope, and it sounds like they're planning to break in and get it."

Miles paused with his hand reaching for the letter opener on his desk.

"How do you know all this?"

"We're listening to the conversation in their car via Dominic's mobile phone. I set it up with an eavesdrop short code before he left this evening."

"Young man, we have yet to meet, but I must say your

reputation is sprinting before you. Do you know where they are currently?"

"I'm with Jonathan following them along the A40. We're heading east into central London, and we've just passed Northolt airfield. I reckon they could be with you in thirty minutes. Maybe less."

Miles picked up a large ball of rubber bands from his desk and began turning it over and over in his hand.

"Who's in the car with poor Dominic?"

"There's a man called Randolph James...."

"The MP who lives upstairs to Dominic? Have they kidnapped him as well?"

"No, Mr. Torrington. He's one of the creeps."

Miles stopped rolling the ball of rubber bands abruptly and laid it down. "Good God, I can't believe it."

"That's what they seem to be banking on, sir. There's a woman called Janet Downpatrick with him...."

"I've heard of her. Merchant banker with a mouth. A chum of mine acted for her when she sacked a woman employee who was pregnant. Seems that she's opposed to equality for women in the workplace. Even though she herself climbed atop the greasy pole. Halfway through the hearing, she started mouthing off to the press about how women should put family before their careers. Didn't help her case much. My chum who was defending her was very put out. Is it just the two of them with Dominic?"

"They've got a driver called Viktor. Foreign accent. Maybe Russian or Ukrainian. He seems to be some kind of security expert from what they've been saying. Presumably he's going to bust your safe open."

Harrison walked in with the tray of coffee and set it down on the desk.

"Heard of some Russian fellah called Viktor in the world of security, Harrison?"

"I 'ope you don't mean Viktor Krasov. Bit of a butcher by all accounts. What's 'e done?"

"If it is him, he's heading this way with a couple of his friends who've kidnapped Mr. Delingpole. It seems they're after this." Miles held up the envelope. "We'll have to place it out of their reach before they arrive." He picked up the ball of rubber bands and began to roll it vigorously once more. "Then again, they've got Dominic in tow. If the envelope's gone when they get here, we have no idea what sort of unspeakable things they might do to him. He's their hostage."

Harrison began pouring the coffee. "But if they find it, they might decide they have no more use for Mr. Delingpole."

"You think they'd do him in? It's a possibility. Steve, how accurately are you able to track Dominic with your gadgets?"

"It depends on signal strengths and all sorts of other factors. Could be within a few feet if there are lots of Wi-Fi sources around. It's better if we keep them within sight."

Harrison set down the coffeepot and handed Miles a cup. "Might I suggest, sir, that we make a copy of the data card and then put the envelope back in the safe? We already 'ave copies of everythin' else. Let them believe they've got away with it, and then we simply leave the police to pull the car over. I've got a contact in the City of London Police who can set that up for us."

"Capital idea! Steve, give us the number plate of the car Dominic's in. We've got it all organized at this end. Just make sure they don't spot you following them. Their driver chappie isn't pleasant by all accounts."

25

JOHN AND Jay ran into the main entrance of the hospital and collapsed onto a row of plastic seats near the doors, grinning at each other as they caught their breath. An elderly couple sitting opposite stared at them disapprovingly. A low buzz of chatter in the reception area emanated from the twenty or so people milling around. Some were aimlessly browsing the newsstand and sandwich shop; others sat chatting quietly in corners, blankly watching the medical staff hurrying by.

John looked down to see splashes of scarlet oozing from his hand and dripping onto the floor. There was a deep cut around the base of his thumb. He must have caught it on the van door. As he pulled out a grubby handkerchief from his pocket, his mobile phone fell onto the floor. Picking it up, he stared at the screen.

"Damn, the battery's died. I'm going to have to charge it and get back in touch with Steve so he knows I'm okay."

"Hang on a minute, mate. Don't you think you should get that hand of yours checked out first? We're in the right place."

John shoved the phone back in his pocket.

"It's nothing. It'll stop bleeding in a minute." He briefly examined the bloodied hand and began winding his handkerchief around it. "Shit, was I pleased to see you, Jay! So were you inside the house when they started smashing their way in?"

"No, mate. I was down the road when I saw them start on the door. I ducked out the way, not knowing what the fuck was going on. Then those bastards came running out and drove off in the van. I ran after them and kept up all the way to the main road. That's when I saw you come out of the Eagle pub. They started tailing you from there." Jay stood up. "Where's Gemma? Should we go back and check for her?"

"No, I don't reckon she's at the house yet. Still on her way back from London. She took that stuff up to meet the lawyer guy. Did you get the number plate of the van, by the way?"

Jay looked smug.

"Sure did. And I reckon I could describe the two guys. Should we call the police?"

John finished winding the grubby handkerchief around his hand and stood up.

"I don't know who we can trust anymore. For all we know, they could have *been* the police. I think our best hope is Mr. Delingpole. He seems to be on our side. Let's go up and see Simon. Then we'll try and get hold of Gemma and see how she got on."

THE ATMOSPHERE in the Mercedes was hot and oppressive. Dominic shifted uncomfortably in his seat. He watched the familiar sights of the Marylebone Road, one of London's main arteries, go past. The Landmark Hotel, Baker Street, the Planetarium, Madame Tussaud's waxworks—the car left them all behind as it headed on towards Euston Road before turning off towards Holborn and Lincoln's Inn, the ancient heart of England's legal profession.

Dominic tried once again to loosen the seat belt buckle at his side, but it was impossible to free. He was strapped into the seat by a webbing harness that crossed both his shoulders and fitted tightly around his waist. There was no way he could slip out of it. He looked across at the face of Janet Downpatrick, lit by the yellow street lamps. She was an attractive woman in her early thirties. Her auburn hair was scraped tightly away from her face, but a cashmere scarf around her neck softened her features and made her appear less threatening. Until she spoke.

"Viktor, I think it's time we resolved the outstanding issue of the Gregory boy. He's the reason we're chasing around London at this time of night. Freedman was useless. Two attempts and he bungled it both times."

"With respect, ma'am," the man called Viktor said slowly and deliberately, as though choosing his words with care. "Freedman was acting under Mr. James's instructions to use ketamine. I did advise that he would be unreliable. He was simply a junior researcher, recruited to the cause and eager to please. Not a competent killer at all."

Randolph James looked across at Viktor. "Krasov, there was no need for him to be killed. He was a bloody good researcher."

Janet Downpatrick leaned forward and placed a hand on the MP's shoulder. "Don't be so sentimental, Randolph. You'll find another one. He was just another necessary death for the cause."

A necessary death. The phrase spun around in

Dominic's head as he rapidly pieced together the new information.

So Peter Freedman's death outside the Brighton sauna had not been an accident. The driver of the black Range Rover that hit Freedman was working for Viktor. Dominic remembered the police had said the driver's name was Faldon. He thought again about Miles Torrington's theory that the ambulance crew who turned up that night had been fake. Miles was right. If these people had those kinds of resources, Dominic could only hope that Steve was able to hear all of this chilling conversation and get to the police before anything else happened to Simon.

Krasov turned the car down Woburn Place and headed towards Russell Square. Dominic calculated that they were about five minutes from Lincoln's Inn. Janet Downpatrick sat back in her seat and looked at the driver in the rear-view mirror.

"Viktor, your man seemed to do a good job with Freedman. Can we use him for the Gregory boy?"

"Ma'am. Faldon is already briefed and ready to go. There's always a police officer on duty outside the boy's door, since they stepped up security. The next shift change is at eleven tonight. Faldon has a police uniform, even a radio, which he can monitor to be sure the hospital security doesn't get wise to him. We just need your go-ahead. Then the officer due to go on shift can be dealt with and our man will take his place at eleven. He's going to have many opportunities during the night. Apparently now that the boy's recovered consciousness, the mother isn't there all night."

Janet Downpatrick looked across at Dominic and her mouth twisted into a smile as she replied. "Tell him to go ahead. And make sure it's third time lucky."

JONATHAN FIDGETED as Steve called John's number again and waited while the voice mail message recited its mantra.

"John, it's Steve here. Ring me as soon as you get this message. Simon's going to be in serious danger from eleven tonight. Get back to me as soon as you can." He shoved the phone back in his jacket pocket and turned to Jonathan. "I'm not getting any trace from his phone, so the battery must be dead. Last thing I had was a text nearly an hour ago. I hope he's okay."

Jonathan leaned forward to Pat the Pecs and laid his hand on the man's muscular upper arm. "I think we're going to need you to show off just how good your driving is in a short while. Do you think you're up for it?"

Pat nodded. "Rally driving's my thing. I do a bit of chauffeuring to pay for it. Do you want me to cut them off at some point?"

"No, no. We definitely don't want to draw attention to ourselves for the moment. Mr. Delingpole's in the back of that car, and we don't want them doing anything nasty to him." Jonathan felt the driver's bicep appreciatively. "My, my, Pat the Pecs. You clearly work out. Presumably you can defend yourself if things get a bit nasty?"

Pat was obviously flattered by the attention and did not flinch as Jonathan massaged his upper arm.

"Yeah, but I'd rather not if you don't mind. This kind of stuff wasn't part of the deal with Mr. Delingpole, and I don't want any marks on me." He tilted his head to one side to stretch his well-developed neck muscle. "I'm a model as well, you see. I've done a couple of ads as well. Is there going to be a bit more cash? I was only supposed to drive you to Chequers and back tonight. Safe pursuit costs a bit extra."

"Dear boy," said Jonathan as he placed his hands on the young man's shoulders and continued the massage, "I'm sure we can sort something out. In the meantime, please don't lose them. Dominic's really rather dear to me."

Pat the Pecs leaned back into Jonathan's hands appreciatively.

Steve was on his phone once more. "Evening again, Mr. Torrington. They're close now. I reckon about another five minutes and they'll be with you. We're right behind. Is everything ready?"

Miles's excited voice filled the car as Steve switched to speakerphone. "This is absolutely fascinating! We found the data card. Harrison managed to open the envelope wide enough without tearing it. Not bad for a man with boxer's hands. Sure enough, the thing was taped inside at the very bottom of the envelope. Just as young Simon informed us. Very clever hiding place. Harrison's copied the data from it, and managed to tape it back inside. You wouldn't know it had been tampered with. Damn clever chap, Harrison. The envelope's now back in the safe."

Steve was looking at a map of Lincoln's Inn on his laptop. "It's a bloody big place, Mr. Torrington. Must be something like five acres. They're not going to just breeze up to the front gate and ask to be let in. The question is, where are they going to jump the wall?"

Miles's voice crackled through the speakerphone. "If you come to the main security lodge on Lincoln's Inn, we can monitor the cameras in there and see what they're getting up to. Jackson on the front desk is a good friend of mine. We always invite him and his family down to the country for Christmas. Absolutely solid chap." Miles's voice began to rise again. "You know, this stuff is absolute gold dust! Your friend Simon has got enough dirt on the—"

A white van pulled out from a side street and shot in front of the Lexus limousine. Pat the Pecs slammed on the brakes. Steve's laptop and mobile phone shot into the front of the car. Jonathan lurched forwards and his nose smashed into the driver's headrest. Pat yelled furiously and leaned on his horn as the white van's brake lights came on and the limousine ground to a halt at a set of traffic lights. "I'm going to lose them. I can't see the car any longer!" shouted Pat angrily.

Steve undid his seat belt, reached forward, and rescued his laptop and phone from the front of the car. He set the computer on his knees and refreshed the screen. "Don't panic, I'm still tracking them here. They just turned off left into a small street after this junction."

Jonathan leaned back in his seat with his head held up, his nose pinched between forefinger and thumb. A small trickle of blood was running down the side of his mouth.

"Have you still got Miles on the phone?" he asked. "Because I don't think we can wait any longer. He should get his police contacts to pull that car over right now. It's the best chance we've got of rescuing Dominic."

Steve frowned as he flicked through several screens on his laptop. "I think you're right. I did have them and now suddenly the tracer signal has disappeared. They turned into Parker Mews and then seem to have vanished. I don't think there's anything wrong with the laptop. Maybe something's happened to Dominic's phone. Either way, I've got no idea where they are anymore."

26

THE INTENSIVE care unit at the Royal Sussex County Hospital was on the seventh floor of a modern tower block. It was just after half past ten when the elevator doors opened and John and Jay stepped into the reception area. The air was filled with the sound of low-voiced conversations from the half-dozen medical staff they could see. From the distance came the dull insistent beeping of multiple alarms.

Jay stopped suddenly. "This is freaking me out, mate. I'm not good with hospitals and shit. Why don't I wait here while you go and sort stuff out with lover boy?"

John stared at his housemate with a mixture of disbelief and contempt. "I thought you were a butch Australian surf boy? All right, stay here if you want. I'll go and see Simon. He's in room 4, down at the end, if you want to come and find me."

He started to walk off, but Jay grabbed his arm. "Hang on a minute, mate. You better get that hand sorted before you go to see Simon." The bright red stain on the handkerchief wrapped around John's hand was growing noticeably larger. "Shit, mate, it's getting worse. I'm going to get one of these guys to look at it for you. Just don't ask me to watch."

Jay ignored John's protests and propelled him over to the reception desk where a young man with curly blond hair sat at a computer screen.

"Hey, we're here to visit Simon Gregory," Jay said, "but my mate's cut himself real bad on his hand. Any chance you could look at it?"

The junior doctor kept working at the keyboard. "This is ICU. You want accident and emergency on the ground floor."

John turned to Jay. "It's all right. I need to see Simon first. I can sort it afterwards."

Jay leaned close into the face of the young man at the desk.

"Mate, could you just take a look at it so you can tell my idiot friend he's gotta get it sorted pronto?"

The typing stopped and the blond ringlets tipped back to reveal a face dominated by piercing blue eyes and a trim close-shaved beard. The young man scanned Jay's broad chest and narrow waist before his eyes flicked to John. He gazed at John for several seconds. Then he stood up.

"Come with me."

Jay hung back at the reception area. "I'll wait here if you don't mind. Hey, mate. Give me your phone and your charger, I'll get it sorted."

The young doctor stopped and turned. "So the eye candy is squeamish? That's a shame. You'll find the coffee machine just around the corner. Bring us something hot. I take it white, without." He grinned as Jay blushed. "I'm sweet enough already."

John giggled, and the piercing blue eyes turned towards him.

"I've seen you before somewhere. Was it Legends or the Bulldog? Come on, let's take a look at that injury."

As they moved past the elevator, the doors opened, and a uniformed police officer walked into the reception area.

IT WAS cramped and stuffy in the lodge gatehouse at Lincoln's Inn. Steve and Jonathan had left Pat to cruise around the area looking for the black Mercedes while they met up with Miles and Harrison. Miles was upbeat. But Jonathan found his optimism false and infuriating. Worse, he wished he had not been so flippant with Dominic, who had always treated their relationship more seriously. It had taken these extreme events for Jonathan to realize how much he loved Dominic.

Steve was swearing at his laptop, trying in vain to get a trace on Dominic's mobile phone.

Miles was scanning the security screens on the wall of the lodge. "I really wouldn't worry, dear boy. Harrison has spoken to his chums in the City Police, and they'll find them very soon. This part of London is covered with cameras. All they have to do is type the number plate into their computer and Bob's your uncle."

Steve was shaking his head. "I just hope they do. I'm confident this laptop is working fine. Which means something's probably happened to Dominic's phone. I hope that doesn't mean something's happened to Dominic."

Jonathan turned and glowered at Steve, before joining Jackson, the tall, balding security guard, to study the battery of security monitors.

"What happens if they decide to break in through a

window at the back of Miles's offices? We'll never see them, then."

Jackson leaned forward and pointed at one of the screens. "You'll see them on one of these cameras, sir. Anyway, if they attempted to break in, it would set off the alarms. Be assured we've got it covered here, sir."

The atmosphere was shattered by the shrill sound of "I Fought the Law" by the Clash. Miles grinned and reached into his pocket to pull out his mobile phone.

"Miles Torrington?" As he listened, however, his grin quickly vanished. "One minute, Miss Downpatrick. I'll put you on speakerphone." He set the phone down on the desk in front of them. Janet Downpatrick's voice filled the room.

"Mr. Torrington. You have something of ours, and we would like it back. Now, we could remove it from your safe. But it would be far simpler if you were to do that for us. You can hand it over to me in ten minutes at that security lodge where you are currently standing."

Miles laughed. "I have no idea what you're talking about, but if you're threatening to break into my chambers, then our wonderful security staff here will make certain you're handed over to the boys in blue straight away. You and your chum Randolph James. Frankly I'm astonished that a Cambridge University man like him would get mixed up with a low-life like you."

"Don't waste my time with cheap insults, Torrington. We know you have the package. Your friend Mr. Delingpole told us. He's being looked after by our own security man at this moment. Viktor has express instructions that if we don't return within the next twenty minutes with the package, then he should deal with Mr. Delingpole. If you hinder me in any way, then you won't see your friend again."

Jonathan felt the blood drain from his face. Miles put his

arm on Jonathan's shoulder reassuringly. Then he turned back to the phone.

"If I get you your little package, will you take me to Dominic?" Miles asked.

"Yes. He'll be released straightaway. We're not unreasonable people, Mr. Torrington. But we don't tolerate theft. You have something that is ours, and we want it back."

Miles laughed again. "I don't think your moral framework is in the same universe as ours, Miss Downpatrick. Don't even begin with your petty self-justification. I'll meet you here in ten minutes with the package."

Miles reached for the phone and ended the call. His hand was shaking, and his face was white with fury. "What a vile woman," he said quietly. "You had all that recorded, presumably, Harrison? I'll go and retrieve the envelope from the safe, and you'd better come with me in case they're lying in wait."

Jonathan leaned heavily against the wall behind him. "You don't believe for a minute that they'll hand over Dominic once they've got the package, do you?"

Miles picked up his phone. "I don't know. I'd rather not believe that they'd kill him. For your sake." He turned to the security guard who was watching the screens. "They can't be far from here. Do you have any view of the perimeter roads?"

"We do, sir, but I've not seen any activity in the last ten minutes or so. It's very quiet out there."

"Fuck! Why didn't I think of it before?" Steve stood up suddenly and punched the wall. "The last place the trace of the car showed up was Parker Mews. I've only just thought to check it out. There's an underground car park there. That's where they've got him, with that Krasov bloke. As they're underground, his phone signal isn't getting through."

SIMON WAS dozing. His eyelids occasionally flickered open and he gazed at his mother where she sat beside his bed. Samantha had stayed at his side in the hope that he might wake long enough for them to have another conversation. She felt that in a curious way, this crisis had the potential to bring them closer together again. Setting down her book, she rubbed her eyes. She had been reading the same page for the last five minutes.

Samantha decided to wait another twenty minutes, not wanting to tear herself away from Simon's side in case she missed the moment when he woke up again.

Through the window she could see a uniformed police officer walking down the corridor towards the room. She looked at her watch. It was ten to eleven. He must have come for the shift change. She watched as he started chatting with the other officer on duty. They were laughing and joking together.

After a moment the door opened, and the newly arrived officer looked in. He removed his peaked cap and saluted her. She felt flattered.

"Evening, ma'am. Are you staying much longer tonight? If so, one of us can go and get you a cup of tea if you want." Samantha thought the man rather attractive. He was tall and well built, bald, and there was a small tattoo of an eagle on the side of his neck. He was a Londoner by the sound of his accent. East End, she guessed.

"That's very kind of you. Yes, please. It's so good of you to look after Simon like this. I was just thinking that it must be very boring, standing out there in the corridor hour after hour."

Samantha stood up and smoothed down the creases in

her skirt and blouse. Her hair must look a mess, she thought, and she really needed to get a shower.

The officer looked past her at the sleeping form of Simon.

"Oh, don't worry about me. He's had a tough time, I hear, missus. You'd think he'd be safe in a hospital. They're supposed to be looking after you." He looked back at Samantha. "Don't you fret, ma'am. He's in safe hands with me here. I'll get you some tea and then you can set off home and get some shut-eye. I'll take care of your son tonight."

27

"THAT'S GOING to need some stitches in it, my friend." The curly-haired blond doctor turned John's injured hand over gently and examined it. They were in a small treatment room off the main corridor. John sat on the edge of a high, padded trolley, his legs swinging a few inches above the floor. He was angry with himself for being here, rather than at Simon's side, and he wanted the consultation to end as quickly as possible.

The young doctor looked up at John without letting go of his injured hand. "Don't look so worried. I'll give you a local anaesthetic, and you won't feel a thing." He paused for few seconds, staring into John's eyes. "I do remember where I've seen you before. It was the Bulldog. Just a few nights ago. You were in there with a skinhead wearing Grinder boots. Not my kind of thing, really, but he had a sweet face. Are you an item?"

John was beginning to feel light-headed and slightly queasy. Perhaps it was the oppressive warmth in the hospital, or the smell. Or maybe he had lost more blood than he thought. Either way, he was not in the mood to be picked up by a doctor who was supposed to be treating him, cute as he was.

He pulled his hand away and tried to get off the trolley and stand up. His head seemed to fill with cotton wool, and his legs buckled as his feet touched the floor. Two strong arms grabbed him around the waist and expertly transferred him to a chair.

"No need to swoon on my account, my sweet. Here, put your head between your knees for a moment. I'll do the same for you one day. I don't think you're in any fit state just now, so it wouldn't be ethical for me to take advantage of you, much as I'd like to."

As the blood began to surge back into his head, John felt a curious mix of emotions and an overwhelming sense of fatigue.

The doctor was really very cute, but Simon was a few yards down the corridor, and the last time John had seen him, he had only just recovered consciousness after nearly dying. His eyes prickled with tears, and his shoulders began to tremble.

"Oh sweetheart, you've had a rough time." The young doctor bent down to John's side and put an arm around his shoulder. "Your Ozzie friend said you'd come to see young Simon in room 4. He's the ketamine boy, isn't he? So is he your man? He's very sweet but a very silly boy to go playing with that shit. Let's get you sewn up, and then you can go and give him a big hug. I think it will do him the power of good."

STANDING IN his dimly lit office, Miles searched through the documents in the safe once more. He knew it was a pointless exercise. The envelope was gone. There had been no sign of a break-in when he arrived. The lights were off, the alarm was on, and everything was in its place. Until the moment he had opened the safe a few moments ago, he had suspected nothing. He picked up his mobile phone.

"Harrison, am I going mad here? You did put that envelope in the safe after copying the photographs and the data card, didn't you? Because it's certainly not here now."

There was a pause at the other end of the phone. Then Harrison responded, "We're just checking the security camera that's pointing at the front door of the offices. I think we may be the victims of a very professional burglary, sir."

In the background, Miles could vaguely hear Jackson, the security guard, talking to Harrison. "I've just spooled through the video recording of the last five minutes. There's nothing been recorded. Not even of Mr. Torrington entering the building. It looks like camera thirteen has been sending a freeze-frame for at least the last half an hour, maybe more. I'm going to have to check the other cameras on the network. Our security has been compromised."

Harrison's voice came over the phone's loudspeaker. "Mr. Torrington. It appears we've been burgled by people who clearly know what they're doing. They've fixed the cameras and the alarms. And they knew how to get into that safe. Is anything else missing?"

Miles walked back up the stairs to his office, switching on lights as he went. As far as he could see, nothing was out of place. He was a fastidious man and he kept his desk and office almost obsessively tidy. It was a characteristic he shared with Dominic.

"You're going to have to come in here, Harrison. Only you will know for certain if anything else has been taken. As far as I can see it all looks exactly as we left it earlier." Miles sank into the leather armchair by his desk. "So who broke in? It can't be that ghastly Downpatrick woman and her cronies. Otherwise why would she go to the trouble of ringing me up and sending me on this wild goose chase? The problem now is, without that envelope, how are we going to bargain for dear Dominic's life?"

Harrison coughed at the end of the phone. "Mr. Torrington, would you be so kind as to go into the storeroom and open the large box of toilet paper?"

———

DOMINIC TENSED as Krasov opened the passenger door and leaned in. He could smell Krasov's overly sweet aftershave, mixed with sweat and stale garlic. The heavily built man checked the webbing belts holding Dominic tight in the backseat.

"He's not going anywhere for the moment, ma'am. Do you want me to stay here with him, or watch your back again up top?"

Janet Downpatrick was standing by the side of the car, hugging her black overcoat tightly against the chill of the underground car park. She had returned from the car park entrance, where she had gone to call Miles on her mobile phone five minutes before.

"I'd prefer that both you and Randolph stay close during the transaction. I don't believe they'll try anything foolish at this stage. But you'll need us out of the car if they fail to deliver and you have to deal with Delingpole."

Dominic's body began shaking, and it was not just from the chill of the winter air. Krasov finished his inspection and gave Dominic a white-toothed smile. Then he closed the door, and Dominic heard it lock immediately. Randolph

James was unbuckling his seat belt as he turned to look at Dominic.

"I'm very sorry, old boy. You must understand that I really don't enjoy being involved in all this. I don't think you realize just what you got yourself involved in. What we're doing is for the greater good. I don't relish the thought of anyone, least of all you, being part of the collateral damage."

Before Dominic could reply, Randolph James MP climbed out of the car, slammed the door, and was gone.

Dominic watched the three figures walk towards the exit ramp for a moment before reaching into his pocket for his phone. He had to call John to warn him about Simon's killer. But looking at the screen on his phone, it was clear that the thick concrete walls below ground blocked any possibility of a signal. He tugged hard at the webbing straps across his chest without success before looking around the car for anything that could help him get free.

STEVE AND Jonathan crouched down behind a row of cars parked in an unlit side street. A few yards away on the other side of the road, Janet Downpatrick strode towards Lincoln's Inn with Randolph James at her side. Viktor Krasov followed a few paces behind, occasionally glancing into the shadows on either side.

Jonathan leaned close to Steve and whispered in his ear, "So that's Krasov. I wouldn't like to bump into him in an unlit street late at night."

As Krasov reached the corner with Lincoln's Inn, he stopped and turned, staring in the direction of Jonathan and Steve's makeshift hiding place. Jonathan held his breath for what seemed an age before Krasov finally turned and resumed walking until he disappeared out of sight.

"Shit, Jonathan. Can't you ever keep quiet?" Steve tentatively stood up and leaned against the wall behind him.

Jonathan ignored the criticism and continued in a whisper. "Well done for finding the underground car park. Looks like this is our chance. They must have left Dominic on his own. This is going to be easier than we thought."

"I'm not counting any chickens too early, mate. They must be pretty confident that he's not going to escape if they've left him alone. Either that or they've already done something to him."

Jonathan stood up and put his mouth close to Steve's ear again. "If you can't say anything positive, don't say anything at all. That's my friend, partner, and lover you're talking about. I don't want to hear any thoughtless speculation from you." With that Jonathan strode off towards the entrance to the car park.

MILES TORRINGTON was momentarily thrown by Harrison's bizarre request. "I presume that at this particular moment of crisis, you're not asking me to restock the toilets. Is this an alternative secure storage box?"

"You guessed right, sir. It's not somethin' I do regularly, of course. But given these exceptional circumstances, I thought it wise—"

"You thought it very wise, old boy. Hurrah for Harrison!" Miles picked up his phone and hurried down the stairs to the storeroom. "So you didn't put the envelope in the safe at all?"

"Oh yes, sir. I put an extremely good copy in the safe. But

you'll find the original, together with another copy, in the bottom of the toilet roll box. I always think it's wise to keep the original."

Miles had reached the storeroom and tipped a few dozen toilet rolls out of a large brown cardboard box onto the floor. Tumbling out behind them came two large brown envelopes.

"Bingo. I'll bring both across to the lodge and give that Downpatrick woman the copy when she turns up. Presumably the burglars who raided our safe won't take long to realize they've got a copy?"

"Given the level of professionalism they've shown so far, no time at all, sir. Which means they know they've got a bit more housecleaning to do. And that's a bit of a worry."

28

BLOOD WAS seeping into the cuffs of Dominic's dress shirt, but he ignored it as he sawed away at the webbing strap around his waist. Thread by thread, the torn edge of the soft-drink can was slowly shredding the bonds that imprisoned him. It took several minutes to sever a single strand of the strap. Often the makeshift saw slipped in his bloodied hand, but Dominic grimly persevered. It had taken twenty minutes to get a little under halfway through.

Dominic worried that the soft metal would not last the punishment he was giving it. From time to time, he glanced around the inside of the Mercedes, hoping to find a better replacement tool for his task, but there was none.

The growing tear in the webbing flexed a little wider as another thread surrendered to the onslaught of the blunt instrument. Each moment of progress gave Dominic a small surge of adrenaline. He was proud of the resourcefulness he had demonstrated. After all, he was the least practical-minded country lawyer in England.

A shadow flickered across the headrest in front of him. Dominic froze. Was it Krasov returning unexpectedly? He slowly pushed the remnants of the soft-drink can under his thigh, too terrified to turn around. The shadow flickered again, and then there was a banging at the side window.

"Dominic! Your knight upon a fiery steed is here. Well, a white Lexus actually. With the very sexy Pat the Pecs not far behind we hope. All is not lost."

Jonathan's broad grin seemed to fill the window at Dominic's side, and he fell back in the seat with relief. "What kept you?" was all he could muster as he looked back with fondness at his partner.

"If you will insist on running off with strange men, don't expect me to be there to pick up the pieces each time." Jonathan was tugging at the door handle. "Now be a sweetheart and unlock this door. It's time we went home."

Dominic tried to reach forward for the master unlock switch on the driver's door, but the webbing straps held him back. He raised his hands in mounting despair to Jonathan outside the window.

"Don't worry, my love. I'll break in. I'm sure I can find something to force the door open. Soon have you out."

Miles had just returned to the security lodge when his phone rang. "Mr. Torrington. We presume you have the package? Please step outside and head back towards Kingsway. We'll meet you now."

The soft Irish voice was unmistakable and chilling in its command. "Oh, and please be alone. You don't want anything to happen to Delingpole." The call ended abruptly.

Miles looked at the security guard. "Do you have those

cameras working again? I'd feel happier if somebody was watching my back."

"No, sir, I'm afraid not. The engineers seem to be a little slow in coming out on a Saturday night. Bit like plumbers, it seems."

"Remind me to take it up with the property management company. That's if I return." Miles gave a mock salute to the security guard and stepped out of the lodge into the chill of the night. This was far worse than appearing before any High Court judge, he reflected.

He had only walked a few paces down Serle Street, when he saw three figures pull out of an alleyway. A large man with a shaven head strode towards him. Miles had little doubt of his identity.

"Wait there," said Krasov. "Face the wall and put your arms up high. Spread your legs and stand still."

Miles did as he was commanded. Krasov stood behind him and began frisking him. Finally he reached up and took the envelope from Miles's hand.

"Stay there and don't move."

From the corner of his eye, Miles saw the woman of the group take the envelope from Krasov's hand.

"So you're Downpatrick? The high-flying woman banker with 19th century views on women."

Krasov kicked out hard, and Miles fell to the ground, clasping his leg. As he lay still, Krasov kicked him in the stomach with equal force.

"Leave him, Viktor, he's really not a threat. Thank you, Torrington. Presumably this is a copy?"

Miles groaned.

"You don't have to answer. We know it is, because our partners recovered the original from your safe earlier. You've just confirmed that you really are the deceitful lawyer we expected you to be. Krasov, it's time to dispose of Delingpole."

Steve was standing at the entrance to the car park. He looked at his watch. It was twenty past eleven. Faldon, Simon's killer, would be taking over at the hospital. He had to alert John to what was happening. But every time he called, John's phone rang for a moment and then went to voice mail.

He started to walk down the ramp into the car park, pressing redial every time John's voice-mail cut in. He could hear Jonathan shouting for him from the parking level below. There were sounds of thumps and metal buckling. What the hell was he doing?

Steve looked at the signal strength on his phone. He was down to one bar. He paused, torn between going to help Jonathan and carrying on trying to get through to John. He could think of no one else to call. If he called the hospital, they would not believe him, and he would need to get back to the Lexus to find Samantha Gregory's number.

"Steve! Where the hell are you? Get down here now. I can't get Dominic out." Steve could hear the panic in Jonathan's voice. As he started to walk forward, he pressed redial on the phone once more.

"Who's that?" came a faint Australian voice from the receiver. Steve stopped and started to walk back up the ramp. "It's Steve. I could ask you the same question, mate. Where's John?"

"You've been ringing this phone off the fucking hook for the last five minutes. John's getting his hand fixed. I'm Jay, and who the hell's Steve?"

As he got nearer to the car park entrance, Steve could hear Jay's voice more clearly. "You don't need to know. But if you're at the hospital with John, then you've got to get to Simon. He's in serious shit. The police officer who's just taken over guarding him is an assassin. You've got to stop him getting to Simon."

"Shit, mate. It's coming up to midnight now. I think I saw the guy come in a while ago. Are you sure?"

"'Course I'm fucking sure. His name's Faldon, and he's in with the same bastards who—"

There was the sound of a loud crash from the depths of the car park, followed by a shout from Jonathan.

"Steve, help! Dominic's dying!"

Steve shoved the phone into his pocket and sprinted into the murky half-light of the subterranean car park.

JAY RAN down the corridor that John had indicated led to Simon's room. As he got closer, he could see a uniformed police officer walking towards the room facing him at the far end, a Styrofoam cup in his hand. There was a woman standing in the doorway, presumably Simon's mother.

"Hey, Faldon," Jay called out. The man looked up. It was enough to confirm his identity. Jay sprinted, lowered his shoulders, and threw himself at Faldon in a rugby tackle.

The two men smashed against the fragile partition wall of Simon's room. Samantha Gregory retreated into the room and slammed the door. As Faldon sank to his knees, Jay tried to get him into a headlock. But as he wrapped his arms around the man's neck, Faldon managed to land a punch in Jay's groin. Doubled up in pain, Jay rolled to the side and then kicked out and upward with his right foot.

Faldon gave a satisfying yell, hunched over, and clasped his stomach.

Jay scrambled to his feet and turned. Astonishingly, Faldon had already straightened up. In his hand Jay saw the glint of a thin metal needle. Breathing heavily, Jay kept his eyes on the hypodermic, not knowing what move to make next.

Samantha's voice sounded from inside Simon's room. "Call security! Someone's trying to kill my son. Again!"

A terrified nurse emerged from the room opposite and ran off towards the reception desk.

Faldon glanced around at the retreating figure of the nurse. As he did, Jay lunged forward. He pinned Faldon's left hand against the wall and twisted his wrist as hard as he could. Faldon grimaced with pain but held tight to the syringe.

Jay brought his knee up hard into Faldon's stomach, then launched forward and head-butted him full in the face. Blood began to pour from a cut below Faldon's nose. Jay gave one final twist, and the hypodermic clattered from Faldon's fingers to the floor.

Jay reached down to pick up the syringe, then choked as Faldon brought his fists down hard on the back of his neck. Winded, but now furious, Jay again got in a low rugby tackle and dragged Faldon to the ground. He leapt on top of him, then wrapped his hands around Faldon's throat, lifted the man's neck a few inches, then smashed his head down onto the floor.

Jay started to scramble to his feet, but, out of nowhere, a heavy metal object smashed into his back. A searing pain spread across his shoulders. He turned to see Samantha Gregory clutching a large red fire extinguisher.

"What the fuck are you doing, missus? You've got the

wrong bloke!" As Samantha opened her mouth to speak, Jay grabbed the fire extinguisher. "Give me that. Bloody hell! I'm the good guy, right?"

He turned to see Faldon staggering to his feet. As he straightened, Jay swung the fire extinguisher upwards in an arc. There was a thud as it connected hard with Faldon's head, and he crashed back to the floor.

Smiling triumphantly, Jay turned to Samantha.

"See? Never trust a copper with a tattoo on his neck. Especially a British copper."

JONATHAN YELLED with frustration. Using a thin metal strip he had snapped off a broken sign, he was trying to force open the door of the Mercedes. It was making little impact. Occasionally he forced open a small gap. But all too quickly the German engineering sealed it shut again.

He could see Dominic inside, still patiently sawing at the webbing straps restraining him in the backseat. Jonathan felt impotent; his efforts to rescue Dominic seemed so futile. And they were running out of time. He was certain that it would not be long before Janet Downpatrick and her henchmen would return to the car.

Throwing the thin metal strip to the ground, he looked around for anything that might help him free Dominic. In a far corner, he could see a broken lump of concrete with rusty metal reinforcing rods sticking out of it.

The concrete was heavier than he expected. Staggering towards the car, he wondered how he could summon the strength to lift it high enough to break any of the windows on the Mercedes.

Reaching the window on the opposite side to Dominic,

Jonathan heaved the rock at the glass. He jumped out of the way just in time to avoid the concrete landing on his feet. It made no impact, save a few dents and scratches on the car's bodywork.

He bent down to pick up the concrete once more. There was an electronic beep from inside the Mercedes followed by a steady tone. A few seconds later, the engine fired into life. Then it roared and began to rev at high speed.

Jonathan looked around, but there was no one else in the car park. The Mercedes seemed to have developed a life of its own. He looked into the car as Dominic started banging on the window.

"Jonathan! Get me out. The exhaust fumes are coming in! I'm choking in here!"

With renewed strength, Jonathan bent down, picked up the jagged lump of concrete, and swung it with all his energy at the side window. Again, the glass stood firm.

"Steve!" Jonathan shouted. "Help! Dominic's dying!"

Jonathan had never felt so terrified in his life. The man he loved like none other was dying in front of him. And he was powerless to help. He turned as he heard the sound of feet sprinting down the ramp.

"Steve, thank God you're here. Dominic's being gassed in this car, and I can't get him out."

As Steve ran towards him, there was the roar of an engine from the floor above.

"Quick!" shouted Jonathan. "It could be more of those bastards." Together they lifted the lump of concrete high and launched it at the windscreen. The car rocked, and there was a creaking noise from the glass, but it failed to break.

"I've got an idea, Jonathan. Give me a few seconds."

Steve crouched down at the front of the Mercedes, its engine still revving at high pitch.

The squeal of rubber on concrete grew louder as a white Lexus hurtled down the ramp and spun around towards them. It screeched to a halt, and the driver leapt out.

"Pat the Pecs!" Jonathan yelled. "Am I glad to see you. We've got to get this door open before Dominic's gassed to death."

Jonathan watched as Pat opened the boot of the Lexus and pulled out a twenty-kilogram gym weight. "Much as I admire your muscles, young man, this is hardly the time for a workout."

Pat ignored the remark and swung the weight with enormous force at the rear window of the Mercedes. It landed with a loud thud, but the glass held firm. Pat took a step back to add more momentum to his swing. Again the glass refused to give way.

"It's got to be bulletproof, Mr. McFadden. We're not going to break that."

Jonathan peered through the tinted glass of the Mercedes. He could see Dominic slumped in the backseat. His breathing seemed increasingly shallow. He felt sick to his core as he looked helplessly at Pat and then across to Steve, who seemed to be fiddling with his mobile phone at the front of the car.

Jonathan's fury overwhelmed him, and he shouted at Steve, "Will you stop fucking about and come and help us?"

He looked into the back of the Mercedes once more. Dominic's chest was scarcely moving. He grabbed the gym weight from Pat and swung it back with all his might. As he did, there were a series of electronic beeps and a metallic clunk from the car, and all four doors sprang open.

The stench of exhaust gas flooded out of the car. Pat the

Pecs pushed past Jonathan, took out a pocket knife, and rapidly cut through the webbing straps binding Dominic's inert body. Pulling him from the fume-filled car, Pat gently laid Dominic on the concrete floor. Having checked his airway, Pat began compressions on his chest. After nearly two minutes, Dominic gave a faint sigh and then coughed before drawing his knees up to his chest.

Jonathan slumped against the car and looked across at Steve, who was holding his phone triumphantly in the air. "Thank you," he breathed. "You're one hell of an electronics wizard. I take back the crap I just said."

Steve's face broke into a broad, beaming smile. "You'd be amazed at what happens when you do a bit of reprogramming on a smartphone, mate. I wrote that one myself. Doesn't take long to crack security codes for a guy like me."

There was a shout from somewhere near the entrance to the car park, and Jonathan looked up to see the distant figure of Krasov break into a run.

"Pat, I think you're about to earn some overtime."

29

"WHAT'S THE latest on your chums in the City of London Police, Harrison? Did you tell them about where we thought they'd find the car?" Miles was slumped in a chair in the security lodge, nursing the wounds that Krasov had inflicted on him.

"They're on to it, Mr. Torrington. I don't think that trio's going to get far tonight. More importantly, the ambulance is on its way. We need to get you to hospital and check there's no internal damage."

"Don't worry about me, Harrison. I've had worse kickings in the High Court. I just hope dear Dominic hasn't suffered at the hands of that Russian ape. He's a little more sensitive than me."

Miles picked up the large envelope he had recovered from the storeroom earlier.

"We've a lot of work to do on this, Harrison. Those students have given us enough evidence to link Barton Kane with some very backhanded funding from the British taxpayer, doubtless manipulated by that little tyke Randolph James and the poisonous Downpatrick. They must have siphoned off millions over the last four years, judging by the paper trail we've seen on that memory card so far. I just wish we'd got the burglars on video tonight."

Miles looked up at the security monitors on the far wall of the lodge. "When's your engineer chappie going to turn up to fix those things?"

The security guard glanced up from his copy of *Heat* magazine. "It's a weekend, Mr. Torrington, I told you before. They'll probably get here in a couple of hours."

Harrison set the laptop he had been working on in front of Miles.

"I don't think you need worry on that score, Mr. Torrington. Last year I took the liberty of investing in some discreet security coverage for your chambers." He looked across at the security guard, whose head was again buried in his magazine. "Just in case Lincoln's Inn let us down."

On the screen of the laptop was a freeze-frame of the room in Miles's office where the safe was located. The faces of two men could be seen clearly.

"I think these images will be very helpful for the police in tracking down our burglars, don't you, Mr. Torrington?"

JONATHAN AND Steve gently moved Dominic's semi-conscious body from the concrete floor of the car park to the Lexus, where Pat now waited with the engine revving. Jonathan sat in the backseat behind Pat, cradling Dominic's head in his lap. Steve jumped in the front passenger seat and slammed the door. Pat put his foot to the floor, and the car headed straight for the running figure of Krasov.

The Russian veered behind a row of parked cars, pulling out a gun from his jacket as he did. As the first bullet ricocheted off a concrete pillar, Pat braked hard and threw the Lexus into reverse. The car weaved backwards at high speed along the length of the car park as a second bullet hit the wing mirror.

Pat spun the car around in the confined space. At the far end of the floor, they heard the roar of an engine. With the smell of burning rubber, the rear wheels of the black Mercedes spun. Krasov headed towards them at gathering speed. Pat accelerated forward and at the last moment turned the Lexus hard left to avoid a head-on collision.

"The exit's behind us!" shouted Jonathan. "Loop round here." As the Lexus turned again, they could see their escape route ahead. Out the side window, Jonathan saw the black Mercedes cut through a narrow gap in the parking bays, heading to cut them off at the exit ramp. Pat braked hard, and Jonathan ducked instinctively as a bullet ricocheted off a pillar beside them.

His exit blocked, Pat turned the car to the right and down the ramp that led to the lower floors.

As he reached the next parking level down, he spun the car around and stopped, holding the car on the clutch, ready to move. Facing the ramp from which they had just come, they waited for Krasov.

"What now?" breathed Jonathan. "We need to get up, not down. We're fast running out of options." He leaned forward to Steve in the front seat. "I don't suppose you've got some clever technology up your sleeve to get rid of unwelcome assassins with guns and high-powered cars?"

Dominic groaned and tried to sit up. Jonathan helped him and put a comforting arm around his shoulder. "Don't worry, my love. I'm sure Pat the Pecs will think of something. He's got many more remarkable talents than I first thought. One thing's for certain—" Jonathan kissed Dominic gently on the forehead. "—your hire-car bill for this evening's little jaunt is going to be a bit more than you expected."

WHEN TWO security guards arrived at the intensive care unit a few minutes later, they found Faldon the phony police officer tied to a bed frame with bandages and surgical tape. A nurse stood guard over him, holding a large metal tray in a threatening manner.

Nursing staff had transferred Jay to the accident and emergency department to check his head injury. Fortunately Samantha Gregory hadn't the strength to swing the heavy fire extinguisher with any force. Jay had a throbbing headache, and the doctors were preparing him for a scan as a precaution. But it looked like there would be no lasting damage. John conveyed all this news to Samantha, who had been waiting anxiously with Simon.

"Don't worry, Mrs. Gregory," John told her. "Jay's going to be fine. Where there's no sense, there's no feeling. As for you"—John held Simon's hand tenderly—"the police have caught that phony, so once they start questioning him, perhaps they can make sense of what's going on. You're going to have to tell them everything you've found out. You can't be the secret investigative journalist any longer."

Simon eased himself up in the bed, reached forward, and clasped John in a warm hug. "I'm so sorry I put you through all this. I never thought it would get so heavy."

John clasped his boyfriend tightly. "I'm so proud of what you've done. They'll be digging around Barton Kane's affairs for months, if not years, now. That company has blood on its hands."

John gently eased Simon back onto the pillow and sat on

the edge of the bed. Then he took a deep breath and opened his mouth. But his courage failed him as he tried to speak. Simon reached forward and held his hand.

"What is it, John? Is there something you haven't told me?" John looked away. He wished it were someone else who was about to break the news to Simon. He swallowed hard and took another breath. The words stumbled from his mouth.

"I'm afraid the police told me some bad news. It's about Gemma. They say she was killed last night at a station in London. They say she fell off the platform under a train."

Simon said nothing but closed his eyes. Rhythmically he squeezed and then relaxed his grasp on John's hand. Finally, he opened his eyes and wiped away a tear.

"Do you think it was an accident?" he asked. "With everything that's happened in the last few days?"

"I don't know what to think," said John. "She'd gone up to London to meet the lawyer, Mr. Delingpole, and show him the photographs. It seems one hell of a coincidence. They say they're looking at the CCTV footage for the platform. But it was crowded and...."

"This is all my fault." Simon turned his head and stared at the wall. "Gemma's dead because of me. My desperation to be some hot-shot journalist."

John leaned forward and brought his face close to Simon's. He released Simon's hand and reached up to gently stroke his cheek.

"Stop it. If it's anyone's fault, it's down to Barton Kane, not you. That's why you've got to cooperate with the police fully now. Tell them everything. And I mean everything."

PAT REVVED the engine of the Lexus as they waited in the semi-darkness of the car park. Above them they could hear squealing rubber against concrete as the Mercedes approached at high speed. A moment later it shot down the ramp and emerged in front of them. Pat slammed the Lexus into gear, and they shot forward. There was the screech of scraping metal as it caught the rear side of the Mercedes a glancing blow and pushed it into a row of parked cars. Briefly, the Mercedes came to a halt. Jonathan saw the barrel of Krasov's gun at the driver's window of the Mercedes. Then he heard the shot. The windscreen of the Lexus shattered. Jonathan looked up and saw blood begin to spurt from a wound in Steve's shoulder. As Krasov took aim again, Pat slammed the car into reverse and rammed into the back of the Mercedes. There was a second gunshot but the bullet fired harmlessly into the ceiling of the car park.

"Are you all right, Steve?" shouted Jonathan. But there was no answer. Steve was slumped against the door pillar of the car.

The Mercedes remained motionless, its engine ticking over. Jonathan looked through the gaping hole in the shattered glass in front of them. Krasov's arm was hanging out of the driver's window at a contorted angle. Leaning forward, he could see that Krasov's gun lay on the ground beside the car.

Jonathan pushed open his door.

"What the hell are you doing?" Dominic grasped hold of his arm. "Stay in the car!"

Jonathan gently took Dominic's hand off his arm and went to step out of the car.

The driver's door of the Mercedes suddenly jerked open and Krasov fell out onto the ground.

Jonathan leapt back into the Lexus and slammed his

door. "Yes, bad idea," he shouted. "Come on, Pat. We can get to the exit now."

The Lexus shot backwards as Krasov clambered to his feet, his gun in his hand. Pat reversed past the entrance ramp to their floor. Jonathan could see Krasov leaning against the side of his car, aiming his gun at them.

"Get your heads down!" shouted Pat. Several gunshots sounded as the Lexus lurched forward, spun left, and hurtled up the ramp. Jonathan pulled a handkerchief out of his pocket, leaned forward, and tried to staunch the bleeding from Steve's shoulder. As the Lexus emerged from the car park entrance into the London night, he turned to Pat admiringly.

"Did I ever tell you that I find stunt drivers very sexy?"

30

DOMINIC STIRRED as Jonathan climbed into bed beside him. "What on earth are you doing?" he asked. "This is a hospital. One patient per bed, I think you'll find."

"Well, there is only one patient in this bed, sweetheart. The other person is your nurse, carer, and lifelong lover. If anyone asks I'll say that I'm speeding your recovery. Anyway, you've paid for a private ward."

Dominic giggled and wrapped his arms around Jonathan. "I'm very sorry for having got you caught up in all this. It was wrong of me to get so involved."

"Don't be silly, sweetheart. I haven't had so much fun for a long time. More to the point. Neither have you." Jonathan kissed Dominic tenderly on the lips.

"By the way," Jonathan continued, "I've just been speaking to your friend Miles. He's going to put his little forensic software team onto all that data the students turned up. He's certain that Barton Kane is involved in a massive fraud. Sucking millions out of global research funds destined for legitimate research into gene therapy, and using it to pay for their so-called 'gay cure.' He reckons there's a little cabal of right-wingers and religious extremists nodding the money through."

"It's very kind of him, but why is Miles doing that? Surely an investigation like that is a job for the police? Or Interpol?"

"Oh, he's handed over all the evidence to them. But he's also kept copies. After all that's happened, Miles wants to make sure no one tries to cover this up. And he's paying for it out of his own pocket. Says it's the least he can do for 'chaps like us.'"

Dominic laughed. "I've known Miles for years. He might sound old-school, but he thinks new world. The more straight people like him we have on our side, the better."

"You're right. He's a sweet man, and he seems to have a scarily big brain." Jonathan sat up and took hold of Dominic's hand. "So tell me, lover, what would you say if Barton Kane, or some other drug company, came up with a 'gay cure' in a few years' time? Would you take it?"

"Are you seriously asking me that?" Dominic's eyes widened as he stared at Jonathan. Then he took hold of Jonathan's hand and held it up between them. "Look, you're left-handed. Many people say that it's more common in creative people like you. But fifty years ago, they would have tied your left hand behind your back to force you to use your right hand. They wanted to stop you growing up 'abnormal.'"

Jonathan pulled a face, but Dominic continued, warming to his argument.

"I'm serious. Fortunately our society largely recognizes how damaging those sorts of actions were to kids. But what if some time in the future they find a gene therapy to elimi-nate left-handedness? Would we enforce that on all children to make them 'normal'? It's no different. Being gay is a fundamental part of who I am. I don't want to be 'cured' of it. I'm not ill, for God's sake."

Jonathan roared with laughter and then fell back on top of Dominic, wrapping his arms around him. He snuggled close and whispered in Dominic's ear, "You know, that's the most direct statement you've ever made about yourself. You can be infuriatingly noncommittal at times. But I do love you all the same."

As they kissed, the door flew open. "Mr. Delingpole! What precisely is going on?"

Dominic opened one eye to see a flame-headed Scottish ward sister striding into his room.

"Well, I think I can see what's going on," she continued with a twinkle in her eye. "But you've been advised to take things easy for the next few days, and I'm afraid this kind of vigorous physical activity is just going to have to wait. You'll be scandalizing the doctors if you're not careful."

Jonathan leapt off Dominic and grasped the ward sister by both hands.

"What perfect timing! Madam, I require your urgent professional medical advice. I certainly don't want to jeopardize my lover's recovery in any way, but...." And Jonathan whispered into the ward sister's ear as Dominic strained to hear.

The ward sister giggled and a broad grin spread across her face. "That's not going to jeopardize his recovery. It's more likely to speed it along. Would you like me to leave you two alone for a few minutes? I only came to discuss Mr. Delingpole's plans for discharge later this week. I can come back later."

"No, my dear, I would like you here as witness." Jonathan turned to Dominic and sat on the side of the bed.

"I'm sorry, lover, but this whole adventure has finally

confirmed it. I can't go on. I've had it with long-distance relationships. Either we get married, or it's over."

Dominic's jaw dropped, and he looked from Jonathan to
the ward sister.

"Marriage? I never thought I'd hear you say that. I
thought you were happy to see me only at weekends and a
few holidays. Where are we going to live?"

"Together. Where that is, I really don't care. I can move
into your apartment, or you can move into my tiny cottage.
Either way suits me. But what nearly happened to you this
week has proved to me that life is far too short to waste time
on commuting."

The red-haired ward sister stepped forward. "Could I
just say, that was the worst proposal I've ever heard?" She
took hold of Jonathan's hand. "Stand up, young man."
Jonathan obeyed the firm Glaswegian voice. "Now get down
on one knee and take Mr. Delingpole's hand." Again,
Jonathan obeyed.

Dominic was finding it increasingly difficult to keep a
straight face. "Now," the ward sister said, "tell him you love
him, that you can't live without him, and that you want to
spend the rest of your life with him."

Jonathan stared at her, and then looked back at
Dominic. "What she just said, only without the weird Scottish accent. Look, Dominic. Move in with me. Take a break
from that job, which you know bores you to tears."

Dominic leaned forward and kissed Jonathan gently. "I
can't tell you how good that sounds. Yes is the answer, but
God knows what I'm going to do for the rest of my life." He
leaned back on his pillow and looked directly at Jonathan.
"Whatever it is, I know it will be all the better for sharing it
with you."

Jonathan jumped up excitedly. "I know exactly what

you're going to do! You're going to team up with your posh pal Miles and do forensic legal stuff. Solve mysteries. Crack crimes. Put your planet-size brain to proper use doing good."

Dominic laughed. "I'm hardly going to get paid much for doing that. You told me yourself that Miles is giving his services for free analysing the Barton Kane files. What are we going to do for money?"

"Lover, what does it matter? You'll be happy. And anyway," Jonathan sat on the edge of the bed and took Dominic's hand in his, "you'll be a kept man. I'll carry on doing my landscape gardening and the odd chorus bits at Glyndebourne opera. We don't need much to live on if we stay in the cottage, and you can rent your apartment out to get some extra income."

The ward sister moved to the door. "I think that sounds the perfect recovery plan, Mr. Delingpole." She turned to Jonathan. "Even if your intended husband is the rudest man I've ever come across. For your information, I do not have a weird Scottish accent." And she slammed the door behind her as she left.

ABOUT THE AUTHOR

David C. Dawson is an award winning author, journalist and documentary maker, and lives in London and Oxford.

His debut novel *The Necessary Deaths* won Bronze for Best Mystery & Suspense in the FAPA awards.

As a journalist he travelled extensively, filming in nearly every continent of the world. He's lived in London, Geneva and San Francisco, but he now prefers the tranquillity of the Oxfordshire countryside.

In his spare time, David tours Europe with his boyfriend, and sings with the London Gay Men's Chorus.

ALSO BY DAVID C. DAWSON

The Deadly Lies

For the Love of Luke

THE DEADLY LIES

A man is murdered, and takes a deadly secret to his grave.

Is it true the murdered man is Dominic Delingpole's former lover? And were they still seeing each other just before his recent wedding to husband Jonathan?

Or are these simply lies?

This is more than a story of deceit between husbands. A man's death plunges Dominic and Jonathan into a world of international espionage, which puts their lives at risk.

What is the ruthless Charter Ninety-Nine group, and why is it pursuing them across Europe and the United States?

Dominic and Jonathan are forced to test their relationship to its limit. What deadly lies must they both confront? And if they stay alive, will their relationship remain intact?

FOR THE LOVE OF LUKE

A handsome naked man. Unconscious on a bathroom floor.

He's lost his memory, and someone's out to kill him. Who is the mysterious Luke?

British TV anchor and journalist Rupert Pendley -Evans doesn't do long-term relationships. Nor does he do waifs and strays. But Luke is different. Luke is a talented American artist with a dark secret in his life.

When Rupert discovers Luke, he's intrigued, and before he can stop himself, he's in love. The aristocratic Rupert is an ambitious TV reporter with a nose for a story and a talent for uncovering the truth. As he falls deeper in love with Luke, he discovers the reason for Luke's amnesia. And the explanation puts them both in mortal danger.

Printed in Poland
by Amazon Fulfillment
Poland Sp. z o.o., Wrocław

49022348R00146